Paul Kane

The Colour of Madness

Official Movie Tie-In

All Stories © Paul kane
Cover Image © 2020 Loose Canon Films/ Hydra Films RKM
Images & Scripts © (c) Loose Canon Films/ Hydra Films RKM

First published by Luna Press Publishing, Edinburgh, 2020

Men of the Cloth (*The Spaces Between*, Dark Moon 2013)
St August's Flame (*Strix*, Issue 14, February 1999)
Rag and Bone (*The Butterfly Man*, PS Publishing 2011)
Pay the Piper (*House of Pain* site, May 2002)
Thicker Than Water (*Innsmouth Nightmares*, PS Publishing 2015)
The Procession (*Darkness Rising Volume Six: Evil Smiles*, published by Prime Books, April 2003)
Words to the Wise (*Phobophobia*, Dark Continents Publishing, 2011)

www.lunapresspublishing.com
ISBN-13: 978-1-913387-16-7

Praise for Paul Kane

"Paul Kane is a first-rate storyteller, never failing to marry his insights into the world and its anguish with the pleasures of phrases eloquently turned."

(**Clive Barker**—Bestselling author of *The Hellbound Heart, Abarat, Mr B. Gone & The Scarlet Gospels*)

"Paul Kane's lean, stripped-back prose is a tool that's very much fit for purpose. He knows how to make you want to avoid the shadows and the cracks in the pavement."

(**Mike Carey**—Bestselling author of the Felix Castor series of novels and *The Girl With All the Gifts, Fellside* and *The Boy on the Bridge* as M.R. Carey)

"Kane finds the everyday horrors buried within us, rips them out and serves them up in these deliciously dark tales."

(**Kelley Armstrong**—Bestselling author of *Bitten, Haunted, Broken, Waking the Witch, Spell Bound* and *Thirteen*)

"I'm impressed by the range of Paul Kane's imagination. It seems there is no risk, no high-stakes gamble, he fears to take…Kane's foot never gets even close to the brake pedal."

(**Peter Straub**—Bestselling author of *Ghost Story, Mr X, Lost Boy Lost Girl*, and *In the Night Room*)

"Paul Kane is a name to watch. His work is disturbing and very creepy."

(**Tim Lebbon**—*New York Times* bestselling author of *The Cabin in the Woods, The Silence* and *Relics*)

"His stories not only, at his best, put him neck and neck with Ramsey Campbell and Clive Barker, but also in the company of greats like Machen and MR James. You don't rest easily after reading a Paul Kane story, but strangely your eyes have been somewhat opened."

(**Stephen Volk**—BAFTA winning screenwriter of *Gothic*, *Ghostwatch*, *Afterlife*, *The Awakening* and *Midwinter of the Spirit*; author of *Whitstable*, *Leytonstone* and *The Parts We Play*)

"He stands out as one of the better writers I've read."

(*Eternal Night*)

"Wonderfully dark and satisfying."

(*Dark Side Magazine*)

"Kane is best when taking risks with his bizarre flights of imagination."

(*SFX Magazine*)

"Kane is a highly regarded author whose influence can be felt across the genre, with a large and notable body of work behind him."

(*Starburst Magazine*)

For all my friends working in the film and
TV world who inspire me every single day.

Other Books by Paul Kane:

Novels
Arrowhead
Broken Arrow
Arrowland
Hooded Man (Omnibus)
The Gemini Factor
Of Darkness and Light
Lunar
Sleeper(s)
The Rainbow Man (as P.B. Kane)
Blood RED
Sherlock Holmes and the Servants of Hell
Before
Deep RED
Arcana
The Red Lord
Forthcoming: The Storm

Novellas & Novelettes
Signs of Life
The Lazarus Condition
Dalton Quayle Rides Out
RED
Pain Cages
Creakers (chapbook)
Flaming Arrow
The Bric-a-Brac Man
The P.I.'s Tale
Snow
The Rot
Beneath the Surface (with Simon Clark)
Blood Red Sky

Collections

Alone (In the Dark)
Touching the Flame
FunnyBones
Peripheral Visions
The Adventures of Dalton Quayle
Shadow Writer
The Butterfly Man and Other Stories
The Spaces Between
Ghosts
Monsters
The Dead Trilogy
The Spirits of Christmas
Shadow Casting
Nailbiters
Death
The Life Cycle
Disexistence
Kane's Scary Tales
More Monsters
Lost Souls
The Controllers
White Shadows (as P.B. Kane)
Traumas
Forthcoming: Darkness & Shadows

Editor & Co-Editor

Shadow Writers Vol. 1 & 2
Terror Tales #1-4
Top International Horror
Albions Alptraume: Zombies
The British Fantasy Society: A Celebration
Hellbound Hearts
The Mammoth Book of Body Horror
A Carnivàle of Horror: Dark Tales from the Fairground

Beyond Rue Morgue
Dark Mirages
Exit Wounds
Wonderland
Cursed

Non-Fiction
Contemporary North American Film Directors: A Wallflower
Critical Guide (Major Contributor)
Cinema Macabre (Contributor)
The Hellraiser Films And Their Legacy
Voices in the Dark
Shadow Writer—The Non-Fiction. Vol. 1: Reviews
Shadow Writer—The Non-Fiction. Vol. 2: Articles & Essays
Leviathan—The Story of Hellraiser and Hellbound: Hellraiser
II (contributor)
Hellraisers

Acknowledgments:

My thanks to Francesca and Rob at Luna for their undying enthusiasm and professionalism. Thanks to Iana Zaalishvili for the terrific cover art, which was an original poster image for the film, and to Andy Collier, Tor Mian and Barbara Crampton for their help and contributions. As always, hugs and massive thank yous to all my friends in the writing and film/TV world, for their continual help and their support in the past. A very special thank you, though, to people like Clive Barker, Neil Gaiman, Mike Carey, Sarah Pinborough, Michael Marshall Smith, Jason Arnopp, Joe Hill, Kelley Armstrong, Rio Youers, AK Benedict, Christopher Fowler, Stephen Volk, Pete and Nicky Crowther, Tim Lebbon, John Connolly, Simon Clark and so many more. Finally, a massive thank you to my family, especially my lovely wife Marie who helps me channel the madness.

Contents

Men of the Cloth

They say you can't go home.

But that was exactly what they were doing. Well, what her husband was *attempting*, at any rate—and Lance had dragged the rest of his family along for the ride. A ride that was now taking them over the crest of another rolling green hill. Yes, it was beautiful countryside, but when you'd seen one field you'd seen them all. Especially if a *certain someone* insisted on stopping to take photographs every half mile. In spite of also being originally from this country, Shelley had been in no massive rush to return. Lance had only really managed to convince her about this trip by promising they could break things up with visits to the nation's major cities and tourist hotspots along the way, starting with its famous capital.

Their kids, Zach and Amber, had enjoyed that part too. Seeing Big Ben, the London Eye, Houses of Parliament—then on to visit a few castles and stately homes as they made their way northwards. To them it had been exotic, like visiting a whole other world ... which in some respects England was to people living across the Atlantic: you only had to watch the news to see that. Brits and Americans were so alike in a lot of ways, but so far apart in others. Distant cousins who saw each other once in a blue moon, who might resemble one another superficially but found they had nothing to talk about once the initial "so, what's new with you?"s had been dealt with.

And now, ten days into their trip, the original excitement of meeting that cousin had definitely waned, at least for her. Plus, watching DVDs and playing computer games in the back as they drove would only keep the kids quiet for so long. Shelley couldn't remember the last time they'd spotted even a hint of civilisation. Probably when they'd hired out the car and set off for the middle of nowhere in the first place (remembering to drive on the left had been fun). Oh, they'd come across a few quaint villages, stopping for bites to eat—was it too much to ask for a decent burger over here?—and for Shelley to buy nick-nacks, but nothing like the sights her husband had agreed to show them. When they were done here it was on to a couple more cities, he kept saying, but all they'd seen for ages were increasingly narrow country lanes.

She glanced across at him, that same look on his face he'd had when he broached this journey in the first place. A determination to find ... what? Not just the place of his birth, but a sense of who he really was. Maybe that was it? Maybe it was because Lance had been taken away at such a young age, while Shelley had lived over here until she was nine. For her, moving to New York with her parents had been the adventure, a chance to start again after the problems she'd had at school; to reinvent herself, which she'd ultimately done. A confident and successful executive at a fashion house, who'd seen off all competition and gone on to make a fortune in the process. She'd shown those bullies, those people who'd made fun of her family for being poor. Who was laughing now, eh?

Yet as confident as she was, Shelley had still relented about this trip, and wasn't there a part of her that had felt nine again when she set foot back on these shores? Remembering that grotty council estate and all it symbolised. Maybe *she* was going home, too, but in a different way. A way she didn't want, and couldn't face.

Dammit, Lance!

"Is it really that important to you?" she'd asked him when he'd explained the idea one evening, after plying her with gin and tonics.

Lance had nodded. "It's my heritage. It's where I come from. I'd just like to see it one time, is all."

Shelley could kind of understand that. Lance's mom had upped sticks and moved halfway around the globe, but he'd never found out why because she'd ended up developing dementia by the time he was in high school. Lance had found himself in a couple of foster homes after that, until he was old enough to apply for college. He'd visited his mother every week, however—even though she didn't have a clue who he was—until her recent death. Perhaps that was what had sparked this sudden interest in the past? That, and his own kids growing up.

"Besides, I can probably get some great pictures for the exhibition," he'd told her. That was true, and he'd more than likely sell them afterwards for quite a bit of money. Lance Dunham was fast becoming a bankable name in the world of serious photography. The images more highbrow than those he'd been snapping the first time they'd met, when he was taking pictures for a newspaper piece on Fashion Week. He'd looked so cute back then, in his tight jeans and open-necked shirt. Shelley had caught him staring across the catwalk, and was flattered when he smiled at her. *No mean feat*, she'd told herself, *when the competition were all supermodels*. Fourteen years later and they were still together, but things were far from perfect.

He'd changed tack about the visit again at that point, pushing the fact that they could make a real holiday of it. They both worked hard and could use a break; could do with spending more time as a family. Playing the guilt card because the pair of them knew they should see more of their kids.

"It'll be good for *all* of us," he'd said. And she'd known what he meant by that, as well. Between her work on the new line recently, and his time spent at the studio, the kids hadn't been the only ones who'd felt neglected. Their relationship, their whole marriage in fact, was in danger of becoming more estranged than those distant cousins, the US and UK.

So she'd let herself be fooled into thinking it *would* be good for them, regardless of how she knew this would pan out. Now Shelley was bored. *Really* bored. Especially today. They'd got lost several times, been stuck behind tractors moving at a snail's pace, and had to stop for directions at isolated farmhouses and cottages, where the inhabitants either didn't answer the door or looked sideways at them—like they'd just arrived in a mothership and taken on human form.

"Where exactly *are* we looking for?" asked Amber, surfacing from her DVD, pulling out her earphones.

"That's the thing," Shelley had called back. "Your dad doesn't really know, do you?"

Amber groaned.

"I know the general area," Lance protested, shooting Shelley a stern look. "I got a place name from my birth certificate and—"

"A place you looked up that doesn't appear to exist," Shelley reminded him. *And a birth certificate that doesn't name the father …*

"I know it has to be near Haverbrook, because it said: Camlin, Haverbrook. It must have changed its name or somethin'."

"Except we're having trouble even finding Haverbrook."

"Can't you just look it all up on the Sat Nav?" grumbled Amber.

"It's useless in this part of the countryside," he told his daughter. "These little localities are too small to pick up on, Am."

Shelley sighed, examining the map he'd given her when she'd last complained about the boredom. Haverbrook was at least on that, though about as big as a pin-head, but they'd obviously taken a wrong turn somewhere. *Yeah, definitely*, she said to herself.

"I'm hungry," came another voice from the backseat. It was Zach, looking up from the beeps and flashes of his handheld game. Once he'd said that, Shelley realised just how famished she was, too.

"Won't be long now till we find it," promised Lance, looking at his son through the rear view.

"You reckon?" said Shelley.

Lance didn't answer.

"It's almost six-thirty," she informed him, as if the huge digital display on the dashboard wasn't enough. *Dinnertime*, her stomach reminded her with a growl. "It'll be dark soon."

"It'll be a little while more this time of year, Shel," Lance reminded her.

She flashed him a look of annoyance that matched his own, and not for the first time on their little jaunt.

"I'm huuungry," Zach repeated, this time drawing out the words to emphasise the torture this obviously was for him.

"Okay, okay," snapped Lance, "we get it."

"Don't take it out on him," Shelley warned her husband. "I'm hungry as well. I'll bet we all are. Aren't *you*, Amber?"

When Shelley twisted in her seat, Amber shrugged, her blonde fringe falling over one eye in a way that would have irritated the hell out of her mother. It didn't mean the girl wasn't hungry; Amber didn't eat nearly enough, and sometimes Shelley wondered how much her own industry was responsible for that. Whatever Amber did, she would never be like those supermodels Shelley dealt with on a day-to-day basis. But why would anyone want to be?

"That settles it," Shelley said, facing front again. "Next place we find, we get something to eat, and check into a B&B. Then tomorrow, we head back to the bright lights. Agreed?"

Again, Lance said nothing, but his jaw started to twitch.

The next place they found wasn't too far away, up a few more lanes where the trees overhung, cutting out the sun. Then, as they emerged from the shadows, there was a turning. "I can see houses," shouted Zach excitedly, now more interested in the view outside than on his screen. The prospect of food always did get him that way.

Grimacing, Lance turned the wheel. He'd get over it, Shelley knew, especially when they got some food inside them and maybe a couple of stiff drinks. But then, as she kept her eyes on his face, she saw the grimace transform into a smile. Tracing his gaze, Shelley saw why. In front of them, down the lane they'd turned into, was a sign that read simply: CAMLIN.

Unlike most of the villages they'd passed through, the writing on that sign looked handwritten, slightly ragged ... she might even describe it as "torn". Either it was real, or someone had gone to great pains to give that impression. Before she could examine it further, they'd driven past and were heading down into a valley-like dip. The houses Zach had spotted were obviously on the outskirts, a couple of small off-white cottages with badly thatched roofs. People stood in the gardens, tending the flowers that should have been there but weren't; they never even looked up in the car's direction as it drove by.

On into the village proper, through more winding lanes, passing a park with swings, a roundabout and a slide, and a shop not far away from that. They spotted more modern houses—modern by these kind of villages' standards—but not in much better shape. Some were made of patchworks of stone, some just plain brown brick, but all had that weathered look about them. Old and worn out, contrasting against another beautiful backdrop of climbing hills; specks of white and black denoting grazing sheep. More figures were in the overgrown gardens—some alone, some in twos and threes—and it wasn't until they drew nearer that Shelley realised they weren't people at all. For one thing they were a little too small.

"Look at the scarecrows, Mom!" shouted Zach, jumping up and down, his spiky hair vibrating.

Shelley pressed her face up against the window, dropping the map and touching the glass. They weren't scarecrows as such, not meant to keep birds from pecking at seed in the fields. No, these were something else, something *different*. She took in more of their features as Lance slowed the car, the figures dressed in rags or cloth, the stitching clearly visible; some wearing smocks, some ordinary jackets or trousers. The hands and heads were also made from that same kind of material, faces sewn on, black eyes staring back at them—but not coal or buttons or anything like that ... Actually, she wasn't quite sure what they were made from, though they shone out of those heads like black light, reflecting the sun but turning it into something much darker. She could see no straw or any other means of stuffing, yet the figures were solid enough. Perhaps more solid than any "scarecrow" she'd ever seen (not that she was an expert). Shelley felt her flesh prickle at the sight of them, and squirmed in the seat.

She turned to look back at Lance, who was beaming even more. "It must be some kind of celebration or somethin'," he said, driving along another street and pointing to the stone walls, the lamps decorated in ribbons and brightly-coloured materials. It jarred against the rundown nature of the village itself. A little further up was what looked like some kind of notice board set atop a stone base in the middle of the square. "Maybe a well dressing?" Shelley was sort of familiar with the odd tradition from when she lived in this country, where smaller rural communities every so often decorated areas near to water sources—like springs— usually with flowers.

"I can't see any wells," she said.

Lance didn't take his eyes off the road. "Looks pretty, whatever's happening."

Yeah, very pretty, except for those creepy ass scarecrows. "Lance, I—"

"Let's see if we can find somewhere to eat, shall we? Maybe a B&B like you said."

That's right, she had. But suddenly Shelley wanted to take back those words, wanted to say they'd stop in the next place after this they found—except she knew it wouldn't make any difference. This was the village Lance had come here looking for, this was where his mother had once lived.

"Yeah, I'm hungry," Zach repeated once more.

Shelley sighed again, nodding. They *should* eat, and find somewhere to bed down. Couldn't risk not finding anywhere else out there, having to sleep in the car, in the dark ... But part of her mind was still saying, *Yes, risk it. Please. That option's preferable to staying here.* Anything *is.*

"There!" said Lance suddenly. "The hub of any community!"

In front of them, on the right, was a larger building with seats outside and a tall, painted sign blowing in the breeze. *The Ram's Head*, it proclaimed proudly, with an illustration of said animal above the words. Before Shelley could say any more, Lance was already pulling into the car park.

She decided right then and there that the first drink, on him, would be a large one.

*

The inside was pleasant enough, all wood panelling with old paintings and photos of the village on the walls, and more nooks and crannies than the pub itself had corners.

All heads turned in their direction when they walked in, though this only amounted to a handful at most. A couple of old men were playing dominoes, pints of real ale never far away from their grasp; a woman sporting a blue rinse was propping up the bar, drinking a scotch, and smoking even though it was illegal in English public houses; while a middle-aged couple were sitting in one of the more private nooks, engaged in quiet conversation until these interlopers had arrived.

Behind the bar itself was a man who looked like a retired wrestler, rosy-cheeked with shirtsleeves rolled up his massive forearms, drying pint glasses. Just behind him was a younger woman—a bit *too* young to be his wife, but possibly a sister because she had the same nose, God help her. Above them, hung an actual ram's head with horns that curled round at the sides, either preserved or an authentic-looking fake, with part of its fleece spreading out like a cape. Presiding over the bar area itself.

Everyone watched intently as Lance ushered his family inside. He told them to wait near the door while he went to ask about food and a place to stay. Lance noted the interest the barman was showing in his family, peering over his shoulder to look at the children.

"It is okay to bring them in, isn't it?" asked Lance. "I mean, this is a family pub? Children are welcome?" He knew full well that most of the ale houses out here made their own rules anyway, hence the woman still polluting the atmosphere with her smoke.

The barman nodded stiffly. "Aye."

Lance looked across at the menu on the blackboard to his right. "Would it be possible to get four shepherds pie dinners?"

The barman winced at the way Lance pronounced the dish, and shook his head. "We've finished serving food," was all he said.

"Oh come on," Lance grumbled, looking at his watch. "It's still early."

The barman shrugged and continued to dry the glass he was holding, while the girl behind him laughed. "Okay," said Lance, letting out a breath. "Do you know anywhere we *can* eat, then?"

Another shrug.

"How about somewhere we can stay? A B&B?"

"You're not from around about here, are you?"

"No. But my folks were."

The barman studied him for a few seconds, then turned and regarded the smoking woman. "Pam there could probably find space for you, if you asked her nicely."

Pam looked up from her drink, an expression of surprise on her face. Then she caught the barman's eye and nodded.

"You run a B&B, ma'am?" asked Lance.

The woman with the blue rinse took a long drag on the cigarette and blew the smoke out of the side of her mouth. "I can put you up for the night," she told him, not really answering the question.

Lance turned and looked back at his family. They were hungry and they needed somewhere to sleep; right now "Pam" here seemed their best bet. Shelley returned his gaze, having not heard the conversation. Lance knew she wouldn't be very happy about his decision—wasn't very pleased with him in general—but it wasn't based solely on them needing a place to crash. Now that he was here, he intended to find out a thing or two about his past, and that meant spending a bit of time in Camlin.

He returned to his family, pasting on a smile. "We're in luck, gang. Pam over there runs a little place we can stay at." They all watched Pam downing the dregs of her whiskey, stubbing out her cigarette in an ash tray.

"Great," said Shelley, but he couldn't tell whether she was being sarcastic or not. "And food?"

Just when he thought it might have to be nuts and chips—or crisps as they called them here—from the bar, Pam joined them. "I'll see what I can rustle up for you," she told them, leading the way back outside.

*

What Pam rustled up turned out to be frozen pizza, but Zach seemed happy with that. Amber just looked at the plate as if a hand grenade had been tossed in front of her. Shelley kept glaring over at Lance as she cut up her slices, perhaps wishing it was a certain part of his anatomy.

Pam Napier didn't own a B&B in any way, shape or form. What she did own was one of the houses nearby, and she lived on her own, her husband having "gone the way of all things" some years ago, she informed them. "I'll be glad of the company, actually. Gets a bit lonely around here."

"Well, we can certainly pay our way," Lance assured her, taking out his wallet as they'd walked across the car park. "What would you consider fair?"

Pam shook her head. "We'll talk about that later. You got cases or anything?"

"We won't be staying *that* long," Shelley cut in.

Lance said he'd go and get their overnight stuff from the car, plus his camera bag, then joined them moments later. "I'm Lance Dunham, this is my wife Shelley," he told Pam, "and my kids Zach and Amber."

"Dunham," mused Pam, pausing. "Now that's a name I've not heard around these parts for a long time."

"Really? I—"

Shelley coughed loudly, a signal for them to get a move on, get inside and get fed. It wasn't until after dinner—the conversation being non-existent while they were eating—that Lance brought the matter up again. "You mentioned something about knowing my family name earlier. Perhaps you knew my mom?"

Pam, who'd filled another glass of whiskey as soon as they'd entered her place—a spacious enough abode, but not exactly looked after—regarded him strangely, then said, "You might be best talking to Acton about that."

"Acton?" enquired Lance, sipping at the tea she'd made them all (he liked tea, but could really have used a shot of coffee after all that driving).

"Acton Thorpe, he'd have been acquainted with them."

"And where would I find *him*, ma'am?"

Pam looked at the clock, which said it was almost quarter past nine. "Probably back in the *Ram's Head* again this time of night."

"Really?" Lance leaned forward at the dining table. "Fancy a nightcap, Shelley?"

Lance ignored the frosty look his wife gave him this time, glad that she'd put down her knife, but he couldn't ignore her when she said she wanted a quiet word with her husband out in the hallway.

Pam lit up as the couple stepped out for a moment; both children watched this but saying nothing.

"It's bad enough that you drag us halfway across this wilderness," spat Shelley, "but now you want to abandon the kids in—"

"Whoa, whoa," said Lance, holding up his hands. "I'm not talking about abandoning anyone. Pam's—"

"We've only just met this woman!"

Lance shushed her. "Would you keep your voice down? She'll hear."

"I don't give a crap," said Shelley, stamping like a child herself, but keeping her voice low. In spite of what she'd said, she still knew they had to stay overnight in the woman's house.

"Pam's okay," Lance argued.

"You mean aside from the fact she smokes like a chimney and drinks like a fish? We don't know the first thing about her, Lance!"

"I take it you're not coming over to the pub, then?"

Shelley said nothing, perhaps expecting him not to go either. But Lance hadn't come this far just to let his wife stop him now. Would those investigative reporters he was teamed up with back in the day—before he got landed with covering stupid fashion gigs—have let a thing like this stop them? Shelley was right in that they didn't know Pam, but she'd been generous enough to let them stay in her own home—and they'd only be across the road if the kids needed them. Besides, it was getting past their bedtime anyway.

Lance waited while the kids were put to bed, and although they weren't best pleased about sharing Pam's spare bedroom (Zach in a sleeping bag, Amber in the single bed) they were too tired to put up much of a fight. Then he placed their overnight stuff in Pam's bedroom, which she was giving up for the adults, in spite of Lance's protests (another reason to think the kindness he'd seen in her wasn't a one-off). Lance tried to kiss Shelley before heading over to *The Ram's Head*, but she turned away. After taking a proffered spare key, Lance left her and Pam in front of the TV, watching some old re-run of a British comedy from the '70s ... from around the time his mom had left this village.

"I won't be long," he assured her, knowing that Shelley didn't believe him. She was probably right. He wanted answers, and his first port of call was this Acton character.

Unfortunately, the man wasn't around when Lance returned to the pub. "Not seen him tonight," the barman said. "But that's not to say he *won't* be in."

"Oh, right. Then maybe you can help me, I'm trying to find out—"

"You havin' a drink or what?" he said.

Lance reluctantly nodded. If there wasn't any coffee going— and he wasn't even going to ask this guy—he'd try out the local ale instead. The barman began pouring the pint, and Lance found himself gazing up at the ram's head above. It seemed to be watching him, watching the whole pub in fact. Lance started when a glass of almost black bitter (with a head on it that looked like scum on a pond) was slammed down in front of him. Lance took a sip, not wishing to offend, and found he actually quite liked it. It tasted of liquorice.

While he was waiting for Acton to show, he had a look at the pictures on the walls, paintings and sketches that seemed to show Camlin years—possibly even centuries—ago when it was even smaller than now. Lance took a tour of the photos next. Some were sepia-toned, some black and white, but they apparently depicted the history of the village through its industry: that of textiles. Pictures threw back images of looms, of sheep being sheared, of women on spinning wheels. Drinking more of the bitter, Lance scrutinised the photographs and spotted a name in the corner of one of the later stills: J.F. Dunham.

"Hey," he said, turning to the barman. "Who took these?"

The barman repeated his familiar action of shrugging.

"I think it might have been a relation of mine," he said, to himself more than anyone. "Maybe even ... " Had it run in the family, his own profession? Had his father also been a photographer, a chronicler of life and times, just like he was becoming? Lance drank the rest of his beer and ordered another, quickly returning to examine the photos. In one particular snapshot, the village was decorated as it had been today when they drove in. Definitely a celebration of sorts, he thought to himself. But there were so many people, eating, drinking, sitting at tables lining the streets, enjoying themselves. So many more than the frequenters of this pub would suggest, more than they'd seen driving through the village.

As he went around them, Lance began to see a common thread. In all the photos, during the celebration or not, there were scarecrows in the gardens.

Staring back at him through the lens of time.

*

Shelley was furious with him.

Regardless of how ready for a drink she was, no way would she sneak off to the pub, leaving the kids with a complete stranger—no matter how "kind" the woman appeared to be (she could be a serial killer for all they knew!). Besides, Pam was kind of putting her off the drink. Shelley was also pissed because Lance had gone on his own, to ask questions about his background she guessed. That was what all this was about, really, wasn't it? Not the kids, not her. But his family—his *other* family.

Shelley sat, arms folded, as the cockney man on TV made another stupid joke she didn't understand—because although she originally hailed from these shores, she didn't really share its past, its heritage. Lance didn't either, he just *thought* he did. But there had to have been a reason his mom took him away, quite apart from the fact this place was as dull as ditchwater.

As Pam downed another glass of whiskey (no wonder she wouldn't need the bed tonight, she'd be spark out soon on the couch) and lit another cigarette, Shelley finally plucked up the nerve to ask the question that had been on her mind since they arrived.

"Pam?"

The woman with the blue rinse looked over, eyes rheumy. "Yes?" her speech was slurred.

"What are all those scarecrows?"

"Pardon?" The woman's eyes focussed suddenly.

"Outside, in the gardens. We saw them when we came in. Are you having some kind of celebration in the village?"

Shelley thought Pam was going to laugh, but instead she frowned. "The children," she explained.

Now it was Shelley's turn to steeple her eyebrows. "The children made them?"

Pam nodded.

All part of the festival, Shelley assumed. She shivered, though, at the thought of kids—kids like hers—working on those things. "What was it, some kind of project?"

Pam didn't answer. It at least explained why she didn't have any in her garden; her kids were probably grown up and long gone.

"I know what you're thinking," slurred Pam, "but my husband and me were never blessed, even back before ... " Now it looked like the woman was about to cry.

"I'm sorry." Shelley thought about the effect Zach and Amber being in the house must be having on Pam; thought about going across to her, telling her it was okay. There were many reasons why people drank, the loss of a husband and no kids or grandchildren to comfort her was Pam's. The woman took another, quite large, swig of the whiskey.

"You're right not to want to stay here," she told Shelley, words collapsing into each other.

"What?" asked Shelley, thinking she'd misheard.

But Pam's eyelids were already drooping. Shelley rose, walked over, and took the burning cigarette from her fingers. She stubbed it out before Pam set fire to the whole house.

Shelley sat back down again, looking at her watch. It was

nearly eleven, but she wasn't going to bed just yet. She wanted to wait up for Lance, to give him a piece of her mind and tell him about Pam's advice.

Her *warning*?

But by the time another half hour had passed, Shelley felt herself yawn. A combination of boredom and the journey. "Screw it," she said to herself. And, turning off both the TV and the lights, she retreated to the room upstairs Pam was letting them use. Shelley couldn't sleep, though, until she heard Lance return.

His movements were clumsy as he thudded up the stairs, but she knew it wouldn't wake the kids—they slept like the dead once they'd zonked out—and Pam was too bombed to hear *anything*. He was just as awkward getting out of his clothes and getting into this strange bed beside her. She felt his weight on the mattress, bed creaking as Lance lay down. Part of her was relieved not to be alone, but Shelley was still fuming. She could smell the booze on his breath as he flopped an arm over her. Shelley tried to roll away, knowing what he wanted—what he inevitably wanted when he was drunk. What men *always* want when they're good and loaded, and it was more than a kiss this time.

Shelley shrugged off his arm, but then felt Lance's fingers on her shoulder, trying to pull her round. "Get off me!" she told him. This holiday was meant to be about them getting closer, and to be fair there had been the odd night in a hotel along the way that they'd made use of—but tonight it just wasn't on. She'd never felt less like putting out in her life; the fact she was wearing her t-shirt and shorts rather than a nightie should have told him that. It wasn't just that she was mad with him, nor that he'd been drinking. This bed was Pam's—it really wasn't right. It was weird enough them staying here in the first place ...

Lance's fingers fumbled at her arm, this time tugging. Shelley gnashed her teeth, clenching her fists. "I said, get—"

She was pulled around, and in the half-light from the street-lamp outside she saw, not her husband as she'd been expecting to, but one of the scarecrows. One of the cloth men from the gardens the children had created. It looked even more terrifying up close, those shiny black eyes twinkling in its head, stitched mouth moving but unable to speak past a few grunts and groans. She'd been right, though, about how solid they were—no straw filling in this scarecrow. And Christ, its strength!

Shelley opened her mouth to scream, but nothing emerged. Then she realised why. Like the cloth man, her lips had somehow been stitched shut. When had that happened? Had she nodded off at some point without knowing, without feeling the needle as it penetrated the flesh and sewed up her mouth? How was that possible?

But she had no more time to ask questions, because the cloth man was pulling her completely over so she was flat on her back, then straddling her, wrapping its chubby and tatty cloth hands around her throat.

If she hadn't been able to scream before, then she certainly couldn't now. Shelley did the only thing she was able to, thrashed around on the bed, attempting to throw this thing off, wrestle it to the ground. Her efforts proved fruitless however, because the creature was just too heavy, and too powerful. Its hands left her throat and it clutched her by both shoulders, shaking her and slamming her back into the bed repeatedly.

Shelley's lips strained at the stitches there, pulling against them until at last they gave, ripping her lips to shreds in the process. She could feel the coppery taste of blood in her mouth, the warm sensation as it dribbled down her chin.

And so, finally, she was able to scream ...

*

Lance was above her, shaking her by the shoulders.

He let her go when she began to cry out, shushing her just like he had done back in the hallway. Shelley pushed him away, blinking to try and work out if it really was Lance or not. It was, and he looked worried sick.

"Are you okay?" he asked. "You were having a bad dream or something."

Shelley touched her lips; they were still intact. She let out a slow breath. The bedroom door opened and they both turned. That same breath caught in Shelley's mouth when she saw the figure there, about the same size and shape as one of the cloth men. Then, as the figure came closer, she saw it was Zach.

"What's going on?" he mumbled, rubbing an eye with the back of his hand.

"Go back to bed, champ," said Lance. "Your mom just had a bad dream."

He yawned, and nodded, still half asleep himself. Then he went back out onto the landing. They both heard the flush of the toilet, followed by the patter of feet as he returned to the spare room.

"Shelley, I—" Lance began, but she was at the window, looking out at the shadowy figures in those gardens, eerily illuminated by the street-lamps, checking that they were all still where they were supposed to be.

When, eventually, she returned to bed, Shelley pulled up the covers and scrunched the pillow under her. Though she couldn't blame Lance for the dream, she did blame him for their being in this goddamn place.

And tomorrow ... well, tomorrow she would insist that they leave.

*

Over breakfast, which consisted of whatever cereal Shelley could find in Pam's cupboards—Pam was still asleep on the sofa when they got up—Shelley made her demand. Lance listened silently.

When they'd finished eating, he took her out into the hallway, which was fast becoming their argument spot. "I got to know quite a bit last night about this place," he told her. "The local trade is textiles, Shelley. I thought you'd be interested in that?"

"All I'm interested in is leaving, Lance."

"What, because of some stupid dream?"

"It's more than that. I ... " She couldn't finish the sentence.

"Look, I got chatting to a few of the locals and they agreed with Pam that I need to see this Acton guy. He'll have all the answers about my parents."

She sighed. "Pam herself said last night that we should go."

"What? Why?"

"How the hell should I know, Lance! We could ask her, but she was so out of it I doubt she'd remember."

"All I'm asking for is one more day. I can take a few more pictures, they'll be great for the exhibition. *Please*, Shel. I need to know why my mom left."

He held her hands then, giving her that doe-eyed look he knew she couldn't resist, even when she was this angry at him. "All right, all right. But we leave before it gets dark tonight, okay? Whether you've found this guy or not."

Lance nodded. "Thanks, babe."

"You can thank me by telling me how I'm supposed to entertain the kids while you're off looking for this Acton fella."

"Take 'em to that park we saw," he suggested, "or do some shopping; there's that little village store not far away from it."

Shelley just shook her head in bewilderment. But before she could say anything else, Lance was rushing off to get his camera bag, throwing another thank you over his shoulder. Then he was gone, leaving her to face two very fed up kids once again.

*

Lance began by going for a walk, taking shots of the village as a whole, doing what he suspected his father (?) might have done before him. (But what had happened to the man? The fact that no one had heard the name Dunham for a long time told him the guy was no longer around, but had he just moved on or ...). It seemed to be a tradition, because those paintings and sketches from so long ago—from before photography was even invented—were also signed by people called Dunham. A family line ...

There appeared to be even fewer locals about today; Lance didn't see anyone from the previous night as he explored the winding streets.

He took some shots of the hills surrounding the village next, but inevitably his eye was drawn back to those scarecrows in the gardens. He depressed the shutter, the camera whirring as it took the pictures. Lance zoomed in and took some more, several in quick succession. There was something about them that stirred memories deep inside.

Lowering the camera, he examined the digital pictures on its screen. He flicked through them, inspecting the figures made of cloth. But as he pressed the arrows that would take him back through the sequence again, he could have sworn they'd shifted position. He paused on one, bringing the camera closer to his face. It was standing by a bush, quite a way from the stone wall surrounding the garden. Lance blinked, and in the fraction of a second he wasn't looking, it had moved closer to the wall.

"What?" Lance looked over at the garden in question, but couldn't see a scarecrow there now at all. He glanced back at the camera in time to see the image move, rushing towards the screen. At the same time there was a hand on his shoulder; Lance dropped the camera as he spun around.

He was greeted by a man with a shock of white hair, scrutinising Lance intently. "I hear you've been looking for me," he said, his voice almost a whisper, as he finally withdrew his hand.

Lance composed himself before answering, slowing his breathing. "Who ... ?"

"Didn't mean to frighten you," said the man, now smiling. "I'm Acton Thorpe, and I believe I can answer quite a few of your questions, Lance Dunham."

*

Shelley had taken Lance's advice and walked back up the other end of the village to the park. If nothing else, it would get Zach and Amber away from those DVDs and computer games they seemed fixated on. Shelley might go so far as to say these were surrogate parents to the kids, except they were even plugged into them when she and Lance were around, so that argument didn't really hold water. Or perhaps they were just addicted to them? That was a problem for a whole other time, and probably one a therapist back in the States would be happy to charge them to look into.

She'd somehow felt less unnerved walking past those gardens with her daughter and son in tow, the nightmare of the previous evening having faded, but still leaving her with a sense of unease. It hadn't helped that Pam had told her—in a drunken stupor—to get away. What had she meant by that? Shelley couldn't just dismiss it as ramblings about this not being a place to stay for any length of time—they could already see that, there was *nothing* here. There had been more of an edge to those words ... a truth.

They arrived at the park, such as it was, to find that the swings, slide and roundabout were all in various states of disrepair. Obviously the council didn't make calls this far out into the back of beyond. The roundabout in particular looked so old and dangerous that Shelley wouldn't even let the kids go on it. They sat instead on the swings, trying to get them moving, but not having much success. Whatever the other kids around here made of them was anyone's—

Shelley suddenly paused. They hadn't *seen* any other children during their time here, not even at the park. She had no idea about term times, so maybe they were all at school—making more of those hideous effigies—but then Shelley hadn't seen a school in the village yet either. Something to check on as they walked back to that store, then to Pam's. Perhaps the kids around here were shipped out to schools in nearby towns, maybe even Haverbrook? That would make sense. But then, wouldn't they have seen troupes of children heading off on buses? They had to get there somehow. Come to think of it, they hadn't seen any buses going by, either.

"Mom, can we go now?" shouted Amber, then "Ow!" as Zach punched his sister on the arm. He appeared to be enjoying himself on the swings, at least. "I'll get you for that later, you little monster."

Little monsters ... Shelley shivered, even though it was a warm enough day. She'd be glad when Lance was finished poking around and they could take off. It was just too damned strange here for her liking.

Absently, she wondered what her husband was up to, and whether he was getting anywhere with his obsessive search. *Can't go home*, she thought again, *but why in Heaven's name would you want to call this home anyway?*

Then she went over to break up the fight that was escalating between her two children.

*

His camera was thankfully still intact when Lance picked it up again. "Come with me," Acton Thorpe had told the newcomer, "I've got something to show you." There was a quality to that voice Lance simply couldn't disobey. Acton led him across the village, past the decorated lamp-posts and walls, to the object they'd thought was a notice board when they first came to the place.

It was, in fact, a tapestry: depicting the entire timeline of the village, dating back centuries, and including all the inhabitants. This was the real chronicle of the place. "Since Eve bit into the apple, we've clothed ourselves to cover our nakedness," the white-haired man said. "The founders of this place realised quite how important that aspect of our existence is. Originally, fur and wool was harvested here, but then that turned into—"

"The cottage textiles industry, yeah I saw the photos in *The Ram's Head*. Spinning, weaving, dying," Lance said to him. "But it looked like that business kinda fell apart when mass production came along."

Acton nodded. "We had many good years, but all things must come to an end eventually. Everything comes full circle."

"So how does the village survive now?"

"It exists only to see out the inevitable," was the peculiar answer he gave. "All of this history ... " He waved a hand in front of the material. "It's all part of *life's* rich tapestry. It's all connected, and so are we."

"Sounds religious," stated Lance. Acton didn't look like a priest, but he definitely had that way about him. That, or a preacher.

The man smiled. "Oh, it is. Mind you, pull at one thread and the whole thing just ... " Now he pointed at a name on the sprawling map in front of him. No, not just a name—like all the inhabitants of Camlin on the tapestry, this one had an embroidered face next to it.

"John Francis Dunham," read Lance out loud. The person who'd taken those photos back in the pub; it had to be. And there was the name of his mother beside it, proving what he'd suspected, yet no embroidered face. As Lance looked closer it also confirmed something he'd hoped wasn't true. There was a tiny R.I.P. next to John's name. "My father's dead?"

Again Acton nodded.

That would certainly explain why his mom fled, taking Lance with her. She couldn't stand to be around those memories of her husband, couldn't stand to be reminded of his life—especially as it was all here in the photos, the tapestry. But for them, the story stopped there.

"One pulled thread," repeated Acton. "It was a sorry business."

"Where is he buried?" Lance hadn't discovered any churches or graveyards in Camlin yet, but wanted to pay his respects.

"Later," Acton promised him.

"What happened?" asked Lance. There was obviously more to all this than he thought.

"I'm not sure it's my place to say." Acton looked down.

"Please. Look, I've come all this way. Mom would never tell me."

"No, I don't suppose she would."

"And then, of course, towards the end she couldn't." When Acton look puzzled, Lance told him about her condition.

"Might account for a few things," Acton said.

"I'm not sure I follow you."

"Your mum ... well, she was the one responsible for your father's death."

"What?"

Acton made to walk away. "I've already said too much."

Lance grabbed *him* now, by the arm. "Tell me," he said, half demanding. "I need to know."

So Acton did.

*

Shelley had been right; there was no school in the village.

Or at least there wasn't one that had been in use for years by the looks of things. Like the park, it was rundown—verging on falling to bits, if Shelley was honest. The children of Camlin had to look elsewhere for their education, it appeared. Did they even *go* to school? That had been an assumption on her part, plus the idea the scarecrows had been made there. Perhaps they'd done it at their parents' behest for whatever celebration this was? Not that they'd seen any *parents* either all day. The whole village was like a ghost town.

The store—a very small affair up close, that looked like it just about served the pitiful needs of this community, with a few tins of food in the window, some fruit and veg—was closed. It didn't look like it stocked the kinds of things Shelley wanted to take back as souvenirs anyway, although it did seem to have a good amount of brightly-coloured fabrics: some of which had probably been used to decorate the village, she guessed.

On their walk back to Pam's, they saw no sign of Lance. Shelley figured he'd be back at the house soon enough, once he worked out he was on a wild goose chase. There was *nobody* in when they arrived back, though. Shelley had been intending to pay Pam whatever they owed her, thanking her and packing their stuff up. But the front door had been left hanging open and there was no sign of the blue-rinse woman, hungover or not.

"What now?" asked Amber, still throwing the occasional filthy look at Zach since the fight.

Shelley got them to gather their things anyway, which didn't take very long, then told them to sit in the lounge. She would have taken them back to the car, but realised—too late—that Lance had gone wandering off with the only set of keys. Besides, she couldn't just leave him here, no matter how much she wanted to. Amber repeated her question once they were done. "Now we wait, I suppose," Shelley told her, and both children folded their arms as one.

*

It began to grow dark faster than it had the previous evening, and still Lance hadn't returned. Shelley had fed the kids in the absence of Pam, searching out some fries and battered fish from the freezer, behind where the pizza had been, but it was time they were heading off. Night would be here soon and they'd be stuck in the same mess as when they entered this ass end of nowhere.

Zach and Amber had sat in silence mostly, still brooding over who had won their scrap, but every now and again Zach asked how much *loooonger* their dad was going to be.

Shelley stared out of the window again and, seeing the light vanishing rapidly from the skies, had decided to head on over to the place her husband had spent most of last night. If he'd been drinking the evening away again, then—

She cast an eye back at the kids, not wishing to leave them here alone but not wanting to take them with her, either. In here they'd at least be safe. So Shelley decided to chance it, getting them to lock the front door after her.

"I'm going to bring him back by the scruff of his neck, if I have to," she told them, as she closed the door.

It wasn't until she was outside that Shelley began to feel scared again. Without the kids by her side, or the comfort of a brightly-lit day, the village—and those blasted cloth men—looked even more threatening. Plus the street-lamps were taking their sweet time coming on, too. She picked up her pace, eyes darting quickly left and right, trying to keep track of the figures in the gardens—feeling sure some of them were moving.

Just your imagination, she told herself, trying to shut out memories of her nightmare. *Get to the pub, get inside again. Find Lance, then*—

Shelley looked back over at a garden she *knew* had contained a scarecrow only seconds before, but it was gone now, God knows where. She couldn't help letting out a yelp, racing across the road and virtually tumbling through the door of *The Ram's Head*.

The interior was empty, at least as far as she could see. There was no barman waiting to serve, nor his barmaid wife/sister. Nor were there any customers playing dominoes or chatting in those nooks. The place was as deserted as the village had been all day.

"H-Hello?" she called out, walking further into the bar, if only to escape what she thought—*imagined*, yes imagined—was behind her.

When there was no reply, she ventured even further in, looking behind the bar itself. There was still no sign of anyone. None of this was helping to calm her. Then she heard the first of the screams ... coming from outside.

Shelley put her hand to her mouth. What the fuck was happening out there?

There was only one way to find out, but she wasn't in a rush to go and see. It wasn't until she heard the cries of her children—far off, but distinctive, shouting out for their "mommy", like they were five again—that she came back around the bar. Though not before grabbing one of the wine bottles on display and hefting it by the neck like a club.

Shelley ran towards the door and flung it open.

What she saw was insane. Not only were those cloth men moving—no trick of the mind, now; no way it could be put down to imagination—they were moving *en force*. Congregating around Pam's house. The front door had already been smashed in. Elsewhere, they already had a captive: Pam herself. It was her screams Shelley had heard first, paying the price for the warning. Lord alone knew where she'd been all day, but the cloth men that now held her were ripping her apart like a doll, pulling her limb from limb, spraying blood everywhere.

Shelley felt the urge to vomit, but knew that her children would be the next ones on the scarecrows' list unless she could get to them. Holding the bottle high, she made to run outside, but felt someone grab her wrist. It wasn't one of the things out there causing pandemonium in the village, but rather the barman, who had at last appeared—out of hiding, presumably, somewhere back in his establishment.

Shelley struggled to wrench the makeshift weapon free, but instead it fell from her grasp and smashed on the hard ground of the path below. The large man began to shove her forward and Shelley yelled out in protest. She caught sight of a few more villagers now, only a handful but that included those she'd seen in the pub the night before. They were following the cloth men, the couple sitting in the nook from the bar looking like they were about to clean up the mess that had once been Pam.

Over at the dead woman's house, the windows were being broken, and Shelley could hear more of Zach and Amber's pleas.

Then there was silence.

"Let me go, you bastard!" she turned and shouted at the barman, pounding on his chest. When that had no effect, she brought her knee up swiftly between his legs and he crumpled—enough for her to pull free and begin sprinting across the way towards Pam's house.

Shelley felt something at her legs, then realised she'd been rugby-tackled, as she tumbled forward onto the road. She looked behind to see the barmaid there, grinning wildly because she'd brought Shelley down. Shelley lashed out with a fist, catching the woman a glancing blow on the temple.

Shelley started to crawl forward, aware that this would take her into the thick of the scarecrows, but not caring. All she wanted to do was make sure her kids were all right—she should never have left them in the first place (then again, who could have foreseen this?). But the cloth men were now leaving Pam's home, retreating, making their way towards the centre of the village, towards that notice board thing they'd seen on their way in. And there, standing not too far away from it, was Lance, watching over proceedings—no, damned well taking photos with his fucking camera! Recording everything as the scarecrows and the villagers flocked to the notice board.

Except it wasn't a notice board at all. Shelley saw now, getting up and running towards it herself—shouting a string of obscenities: mainly at Lance—that it was some kind of map or something. But it was quite clearly made of cloth, complete with stitching, appropriately enough, exactly like the writing that had been on the village sign. In spite of herself, Shelley blinked, gaping at it.

"It's the story of Camlin," Lance told her, shouting this as if he was proud of the fact. And maybe he was, maybe this was the heritage he'd been searching for all this time. But how could the man she'd loved for so long condone what had happened to Pam, what *was happening* to his own kids? How could he just stand there and take photos of the cloth men as though this was normal?

"Because," said someone else, reading her thoughts and stepping out from behind the tapestry, "it *is* normal here. Lance remembers now, don't you?" The man had white hair, and was holding an object in front of him: the ram's head from the pub behind her; if she'd been thinking straight she would have noticed it was missing.

Her husband nodded.

The couple who'd been cleaning up after Pam's death approached the tapestry, and Shelley looked on, horrified, as the remains of their temporary landlady were worked into the piece, skin stitched in by her veins, the cloth there practically absorbing it.

The man with the ram's head held it aloft, the fleece trailing down his arms, and other villagers carefully removed the bits of stone at the tapestry's base. Even as the light faded, Shelley saw the threaded veins of the thing were rooted in the earth, the material feeding down into it and pulsating as if alive. The cloth men continued to gather as the ram's head was placed on top of the tapestry, the ends of the fleece working themselves into its surface. Shelley looked across at the scene in front of Pam's house, as if she still had a chance of saving her children.

Lance followed her gaze, then said, "Acton explained it all to me. It had to be done, don't you see? For the village."

"What?" screamed Shelley. "What had to be done? Sacrificing people so that ... what, so the village can flourish again? Is that it?" She was flashing back to old Sunday School lessons about

Abraham and Isaac, about the ram finally getting its revenge ...

The man with white hair shook his head. "No sacrifice. Just events reaching their inevitable conclusion. So the village can at last be *His*." He looked at the ram's head in awe. "So that He can reach out."

"You're all crazy!" she told them. "Lance, please ... " Shelly had to do something to get through to him, they'd warped his mind somehow—perhaps the drink last night?

"We were loose threads, pulled back into the fold. The *folds*," Lance corrected himself, a slight grin playing on his lips. "Don't you see? That's what the celebration was, to welcome us ... to welcome *me* back."

"But Lance, the children."

"Don't worry. They have been given the gift I was denied," her husband said. "When Mom took me away, when she murdered my father."

If he was part of this lunacy, Shelley could see why. Now history was repeating itself.

Shelley clenched her fists and began to move forwards, but found herself being held back—not by the maniac barman and barmaid this time, but by them. The cloth men. Shelley looked to her left, then her right, seeing those disturbing scarecrows, all stitched mouths and black eyes. More were encircling her, encircling the tapestry. She was about to be ripped to shreds, just like Pam, and Shelley felt helpless—she was back at school again, facing those bullies.

But for some reason the scarecrows held off.

Shelley began crying, the tears burning her cheeks. "Please, Lance. I have to go to our kids."

"She still doesn't understand," said their leader, Acton. "They belong to *Him* now. They're his guardians; part of *His* army. Soon, only *He* and them will exist here. And then a new world will follow."

A whole other world ...

The cloth men beside her mumbled something. Shelley looked again at them, at their heads: seeing tufts of blonde coming from one, spiked hair sticking out from the sides of the other. And suddenly she knew that the children had come to *her*. "Moooonnnmmmmyy," the one on the right moaned through the stitched mouth.

I'm hunnngry …

She managed to wrench one hand free and tore at the cloth face of the scarecrow on the left, pulling at the sewn up head. Shelley had to be certain. Parts of the flesh underneath came away, pulling Amber's cheeks with it, leaving a hideous mess of fabric and bone behind. Shelley screamed again, much louder.

Little monsters.

Lance looked like he was going to move forward then, his brow creasing, but Acton shook his head. Her husband was well and truly under their influence. Cut from the same cloth as his father. Dyed in the wool.

And, as Shelley was brought forward, she knew exactly what had happened in this place; realised that all the "men of the cloth" were nothing of the kind. Not men, nor even adults. The children had been turned into slaves of whatever warped god these people worshipped … might even have brought forth themselves long ago. The children hadn't made the figures, as Shelley had thought. They'd been transformed into them.

It had to be done, don't you see?

Over the years, the centuries, these fuckers had given as many as they could to their deity, leaving increasingly less to grow up, to breed—or interbreed—diluting the gene pool until there was one last generation left to offer up and complete the process.

Lance's.

It'll be good for us as a family …

Jesus, what kind of relationship had his mother and father even had, how close had they really been? Related? Had that led to them both going mad? To Lance finally losing it? This had never been about the community going back to its glory days of textiles, that had simply been a cover. Shelley was sobbing uncontrollably, knowing that these people didn't care about carrying on any kind of line, didn't even care about the village continuing as it had. They just wanted to tie everything up and hand it over to that fucking ram so He could …

"We will become one with the great tapestry," Lance was saying to her. "It's for the best, you'll see. They'll even be able to bring Mom back here now I've told them where she's buried. Stitch her into—"

"*Damn you!*" Shelley managed, as the nod was given, as her own children, following some order she couldn't hear, began to strip her clothes from her, then peel her flesh from her bones. Like everyone else connected to this place, by choice or not, she was about to become a permanent part of its history. Its heritage. The birth of a new Eden.

Lance had got what he wanted at last. He was home. It was only then that she realised just how lame her final words were. Lance was already damned, just like her the moment she married him: the moment she bore him their children. They were all just as much a part of this as he was now.

And as much as she hated to admit it, as much as she tried to deny it ...

Shelley was finally home too.

St August's Flame

I had hoped it would wait until I reached the top of the rocky path. However, I was barely a quarter of the way to my destination when the belly of the black cloud above split open, and the first droplets splashed onto my face.

Soon there was a curtain of rain in front of me. It was hard to see where I was going and what had once been firm ground was rapidly turning to slush.

My pack mule bucked at the inaugural rumblings of thunder. Try as I might, I couldn't calm the thing. There was terror in those eyes, pure unfiltered terror—the flashes of lightning reflected in its orbs. For a second I thought I saw something else there, but had no more time to examine them. One of its hooves caught me clean across my shin and I let go of the rein. Almost as soon as I did, it romped away, taking my provisions and tent with it.

I nursed my stinging leg for a minute, then turned around and continued up the path. There was no point chasing after the blasted animal, and to make my way back down the mountainside would be fool's work. I'd be lucky to reach the bottom alive in these conditions.

So I carried on, holding my hand up against the onslaught.

By the time I saw those lights, the sky was inky dark and my clothes were completely saturated. I had to blink twice, working the excess water out of my eyes, before I could believe the sight ahead.

There was definitely a beacon of some kind in front of me; indeed there were several. Miguel hadn't been lying after all. Not that I'd expected him to deceive me—he'd been well paid for his information. It's just that after seven years of searching, seven years of dead ends and disappointments, I hardly dared dream *It* was so close.

I staggered the remaining mile or so, half out of my mind with delirium, until I came upon those stone walls. They were ragged and grey, but had no doubt been standing innumerable decades, maybe even centuries, before I was born.

The stones formed a circular barrier at least twenty foot high, and at the top were the lights I had seen: oil lamps spaced out evenly along the bastion. In the centre was a large wooden door, similar to the ones at most castle entranceways, knotted and thick with an oversized ring on the right-hand side.

I summoned up all my strength and banged on the door. Its knocker was heavy and took some shifting, but the noise it created was worth the effort. If there was anyone here they couldn't fail to notice my arrival.

I waited a few moments, the wall affording me some shelter from the rain, though not much, and was about to knock again when I heard chains rattling on the other side. This was followed by a grinding as—I imagined—substantial locks were undone. Finally there came a creaking and the door was pulled open, albeit only a fraction.

There were too many shadows for me to make out the figure in the crack, but I *could* see his hand resting on the jamb. It was smooth and tanned like a new leather glove.

I broke the silence, trying to sound as pitiful as I could; it wasn't hard.

"Please, I wonder if I might come in to warm myself?"

The person gave no reply, so I spoke again. "I-I've travelled a good distance and must have wandered off the main track. My mule ran away when the storm began and then I saw your lights and ... "

The door opened further and the hand beckoned me inside. As I stepped through, I nodded in gratitude to my rescuer. I could see now that he was a monk. The robes he wore were of sackcloth, and a billowing hood concealed his face.

We walked through what appeared to be a courtyard. Oddly enough, the rain wasn't as harsh on this side of the wall and the isolated building we were heading for was entirely visible. That too was made from stone which had an ancient quality about it.

My guide remained silent as he ushered me through a second wooden door and under a roof at long last. Only then did he remove the cowl. His face was as brown as his hands, with tiny—almost undetectable—wrinkles at the mouth and eyes. Eyes that were sparkling, yet still. His head was shaved closely. In fact, there wasn't a single hair on him, no eyebrows, no five o'clock shadow. His skin was as fine as marble and just as shiny.

More oil lamps lit our way through the corridor. He escorted me to a large room with a roaring fireplace on the far side. The mendicant pointed, but I needed no encouragement. I rushed across to warm my cold, damp body, giving thanks to the man behind me.

But when I glanced round, I saw that he'd gone. Shrugging, I continued to warm myself by the crackling blaze. I watched it slither over the kindling that fed it, spitting occasionally but never dying down. The flames reminded me of why I was here: reminded me of the thing I'd been looking for all these long years. Could it really be in this very place, waiting for me … reaching out to me? Surely it was too much to hope for.

"Would you like something to eat?"

The voice startled me, syllables bouncing off stone and into my ears. I rounded to see a second monk. He was much taller than the first man, but dressed in the same manner. He was without hair as well, and his skin-tones betrayed a hint of foreign blood. Egyptian perhaps? *Please God let it be so!*

I answered eagerly: "Thank you."

The holy man smiled. "I apologise for the reception you received at the gate. Do not think ill of Brother Benjamin, for he has taken the vow. His silence brings him closer to our Lord."

"No apologies necessary. I'm just glad I found this place when I did. Otherwise, well, I don't know what would have happened." I made no mention of the fact that I was actually looking for the monastery, and relief passed through me when the monk refused to press the matter.

Instead he went to a cupboard and took out another brown robe. He placed it on the stiff wooden chair closest to me. "Here are some clothes to change into. I will go now and arrange for hot soup." He smiled. "My own recipe."

Then he backed out of the room, never taking his eyes off me once.

I discarded my sodden garments and slipped into the robes provided. The rough material made my back itch, but at least it was warm and dry. While I waited for him to return I took the opportunity to search the room, hoping I'd find some sort of clue.

There was nothing in the cupboard but more robes and a few sets of beads. And apart from the two oak chairs, there were no other signs of furniture.

Then I noticed the painting on the left-hand wall. In my hurry to reach the fire I must have walked straight past it. But now I had time to look properly, and I knew I was in the right place.

The style was simplistic and yet aesthetically pleasing. In the centre was a man with olive skin. There was a tear rolling from his eye and a bright yellow circle above his head. Both arms were outstretched, as if to embrace some unseen figure. But his hands were flat and turned upwards, a single flame developing on each of his palms—almost like the buds of some strange orange flower. St August!

"Beautiful, isn't it?"

Again he made me jump. The monk was behind me, a tray in his hands and a full bowl of steaming soup on top.

"Yes. Yes it is," I agreed. "Who's the artist?"

"No one really knows," he said with a sigh. "But come now and eat, before the soup turns cold."

I sat in one of the chairs and he placed the tray on my lap. The first spoonful burnt my bottom lip, but I swallowed the thick broth all the same.

"I sense you have a question to ask," said the cleric, inclining his head.

His intuition was faultless. "I was just wondering who the figure was in the picture." I looked sideways at the man. "Is it St August?"

"The patron of our order. Do you know of him?"

"A little," I lied, for my knowledge was extensive. "Wasn't he an Egyptian monk, noted for his prophetic visions and writings?"

"Some say he could see what was to come, yes."

I gulped another mouthful of soup, deciding whether or not to tip my hand. "And then, of course, there's the legend of the flame."

The monk's expression changed. It was only very subtle, but I detected a slight flicker of surprise. "What do you know of the flame?" His voice was little more than a whisper, but I heard his question quite distinctly.

"Only what I've read in old textbooks. That before he died St August transferred his powers to the flame and, so the legend goes, it has been burning ever since. It is said that anyone who touches the fire will glimpse the future. Though," I said, laughing, "nobody knows its whereabouts today."

He scrutinised me long and hard before replying. "It's an interesting fable, my son, but a fable nonetheless. I fear the truth is probably more mundane than history would have us believe. Now, if you'll excuse me, I must prepare your room for tonight. The storm shows no sign of abating yet."

I sipped my soup, watching the brother retreat again. I had unsettled him somewhat, that much was obvious. But perhaps he was just taken aback that I'd heard of the story; after all, not many people had. And if I hadn't stumbled into that bar in Giza almost a decade ago, I too might still be in the dark.

Or was there more? Was he hiding something from me? From the whole world? I prayed that my wanderings were over that night, and that I'd soon find out the answer to my question.

*

The bed—I say bed, it was no more than a flat piece of granite— held no appeal for me. I was too wound up to sleep, even if it had been a cushioned mattress with satin sheets. So for a while I read the bible that had been given to me.

Some time later I heard the sound of footsteps outside my room; the scraping of sandals on stone. Then came whispering, but the words eluded me this time. The noise seemed to tail off down the corridor. Quietly, carefully, I opened my door and stepped outside.

The passage was clear so I followed the footfalls, always keeping a good way behind. It was like a maze in that place and, though I had no way of really telling, I felt sure we were spiralling downwards.

I lost the voices for a minute or two, but picked them up again at the top of a steep flight of stairs. The steps took me down into what must have been the catacombs of the building where yet more lamps could be found, though their brightness was kept at a minimum.

At first I could only make out movement ahead. But as my eyes readjusted I saw the two monks I'd already met, plus at least a dozen more. They were all standing outside a door on the right, the only metal barrier I'd seen since entering the monastery.

The tall one took an oversized key from his waistband and put it in the lock. He turned it, rapping on the door as he did so. I waited, wondering what was going to happen next. Then I heard the sound of a bolt being slid back on the other side. There was someone already in the room!

Surely this was not a prison cell, for the person must have entombed themselves voluntarily. No, the only logical answer was that they were guarding something, keeping prying eyes out.

Eyes like mine.

Once the door was open, there was a blinding flash of brilliance. The robed men all filed inside, heads bowed against the glare. My position prevented me from seeing what was in there, but I had a feeling I already knew.

I crept along, my back to the wall, nearer and nearer to that open portal. As I craned my neck round the corner, I saw *It* for the first time and was not disappointed.

The candle was in the middle of the room, next to a hooded monk who stood watch. It was thick, tubular and white, with globules of wax running down the entirety of its body. And on the zenith rested the flame itself in all its glory.

I could tell just by looking at it that this was no ordinary element. It gave off a red, yellow and orange force that was too vibrant to be ordinary. Too wondrous to be just a thing of nature.

I was hypnotised by it, as were the other monks in the room. So much so that I barely noticed the hand on my shoulder; not until it began to squeeze and I felt pain all along my arm.

Brother Benjamin had somehow doubled back behind me. He was as silent and impassable as ever, his bronzed face displaying not a shred of compassion.

He pushed me fully into the room and the other monks all looked in my direction. For a couple, tearing their eyes away from the flame seemed to pain them physically.

"I-I'm sorry. I—" Benjamin was crushing my shoulder, forcing me to my knees. The tall monk motioned for him to stop and I murmured my thanks.

"You have no right to be here!" he said, his speech more pronounced than before. "This is not for your heathen kind."

"I must have wandered down the wrong corridor by mistake—"

He held up his hand. "Enough! No more lies. I know you have come here seeking the flame. I have known since you entered our place of worship. Why?"

I nearly laughed out loud. Wasn't that obvious? Perhaps not to these simple men.

"I need to know what's going to happen, in the future. I have to know. Please, listen. I'm a wealthy man. I have money."

The friar waved his hand. "Look around you. We have no craving for worldly goods."

"*Please!* I've been searching for so long. You have to help me!" I was close to tears.

He turned to his brothers and nodded once. "So be it. To experience what is yet to be, one must touch the flame with both hands."

I stared at him, afraid to trust my own ears. Was that it? Was he going to fulfil my dreams and let me touch it, just like that?

Apparently so, because he helped me to my feet and led me right to the candle.

"Stretch out your hands, palms face down."

Suddenly I was apprehensive, more frightened than I had ever been in my life. "Have *you* done this before, Brother?" I asked, trembling.

"We all have. Many, many times."

Then my hands were upon it. I could feel the heat building on my skin, but didn't care. My head was spinning. Images bombarding my mind, waltzing over my pupils. The rush was tremendous, like being on a thousand different highs at once, and put my youthful dabbling in drugs to shame.

I could see a townscape, the panorama orange in colour. It flickered like the fire that had transported me there—an effect of the flame, I supposed. The streets were full of people going about their everyday business: working, shopping, talking. I didn't recognise the place at all, but it was much the same as any other.

"Where am I?" I shouted, not really knowing whether I articulated the question.

The ground was shaking. An earthquake perhaps? Cracks were forming in the road, on the pavements, down the side-streets. Large holes appeared out of nowhere catching everyone unawares.

Something was emerging from the cavity nearest to me. It was black and spindly, and as I viewed the scene the most Godless thing clambered out of that pit. Brought forth from the core of our planet, or from Hell. Or maybe both.

Its skin shone in the sun, like armour or the shell of a beetle. And its giant hand clutched the side of the gorge, snapping off pieces of concrete as if it were bark on a tree. Its head was long, with two flared nostrils near the chin. Horns were coiled around its temples, flanking two saucer-like eyes the colour of curdled cream.

It surveyed the devastation, then hauled its gangly frame out of the chasm. Great funnels of molten lava sprayed from its mouth and hands, descending on the passers-by. Men, women and children were engulfed in the red tornado. It blew their bodies to ash and turned pink flesh to charcoal in an instant.

And those who were not killed outright by the inferno were crushed underfoot or devoured by the beast, for now it exposed great incisors at each side of its head.

Yet more holes revealed themselves along the street and soon the entire area was filled with dark fire-creatures. They worked in unison, never needing to speak. It was as if they had some sort of sixth sense, or relied upon a weird sort of telepathy. Together they stalked the highways, obliterating all in their way.

I could see it happening everywhere simultaneously. North, south, east and west. All four corners of the globe were touched in scenes Bosch would have been proud of.

There was no warning. No hope of fighting back.

And though the sights I had witnessed were horrific, I couldn't help thinking about myself. About where I was in all this. What did the future hold for me when these evil demons attacked?

But then the bond was severed. I dropped back, nursing my charred hands. "It's insane! That's not the future. I—"

"You have been shown the truth. All this is yet to come," said the monk.

I looked around at the other holy men. "And you've all seen this? How can you just stand there like that? We have to do something. Warn people. When will this happen?"

I felt a presence behind me. The monk who'd been guarding the flame rose up and spoke. "There is nothing that *can* be done." He pulled back his hood and I was overwhelmed to see the man from the picture upstairs—his face the same in every detail: St August.

"You? That can't be, you're ... "

"Dead?" He grinned. "No. I am merely waiting."

I didn't understand what was happening, even then. I thought I was still under the influence of the flame, hallucinating somehow.

"*What about my future?*" I screamed, my voice echoing around the room.

St August continued to smirk as he reached for the flame and cupped it in both hands. "What makes you think you have a future, my son?"

I stared vacantly at the balls of fire in his palms. Then my gaze travelled upwards to his face once more. His eyes were now creamy-white and skin that appeared suntanned before was slowly turning shiny black.

The monks were in awe, including the tall one and Benjamin.

All bowing and kneeling before their "Lord". St August approached me, horns on the side of his head breaking through and curling round; a yellow glow enveloping his long face, almost like a circle. A single tear trickled down his cheek and instantly turned to steam.

I could only conclude he was an advance scout of some kind, sent to spy on mankind until the time was right to call his brethren from the ground. And his flame? A power source or communications device?

But I found in that instant it didn't matter to me, because I wouldn't be here. I no longer needed that unholy fire to see the future. As St August placed his hands on my head, I could smell burning and I could hear screaming: such terrible screaming.

The screams of a man being turned to ash …

Rag and Bone

When Ted opened his eyes, he realised he was hanging in a room, surrounded by corpses.

Not hanging, as in hanging out—but in the literal sense. Suspended by the wrists, feet dangling with no sense of the floor below them. It was quite dark, and he was only able to see the dead people because of the moonlight, filtering in from a small grilled window to the left. The angle of that moon told him he was underground.

Ted blinked a few times, taking in the shapes of the suspended bodies. They were hung, just as he was, like meat in a freezer. He could see the wounds that had been inflicted on some of them: cuts, savage and unforgiving—the blood now dried in the slits. Some were naked, some wore scraps of clothing, torn away during whatever struggle had ensued before their deaths, or perhaps even afterwards? Some had been so brutally attacked, that he could see bone poking through in places: at the knee in one case, the forearm in another, ribs in a third.

Ted squinted, attempting to make out more, but it was impossible. Some had their backs to him, some were further away, some in corners. The ones closest appeared to be female, that much he could tell. One's shapely legs were in view, and another's breasts were exposed—were it not for the fact they both had jagged slashes across them, he might have been quite aroused by the sight.

Jesus, he told himself, *not now, and definitely not here!* Wherever here was. But he couldn't help himself. It had always been his weakness. If the average man thought about sex every seven seconds, then Ted was so far above average it was ridiculous. It was a wonder he could concentrate on work half the time.

Concentrate now, though. Try to figure out what you're doing here. Or, more importantly, how to escape.

He struggled to pull himself up, maybe try and work his wrists free of the bonds holding him, but it was too difficult. For one thing he didn't feel like he had any energy, perhaps an effect of being in this position for too long? A torturer's potential victim. Because he'd seen this pose before in TV shows and movies, hadn't he. They always did this to the people they'd captured, usually questioning them for information in thrillers. Was that it, was this work-related? Some old business enemy, of which admittedly there were many.

That didn't make sense. Why all the others? Maybe he was the subject of a serial killer. They did the same thing sometimes, stringing folk up like animals, cutting off skin to use for God knows what purposes. It would certainly fit with the corpses who had been mutilated. He tried not to think about it.

Ted attempted again to pull free. Maybe he was still feeling the after-effects of whatever drug had been used to incapacitate him?

He remembered that much: whoever had done this had come up behind him in the car park, silent and deadly. By the time he'd known someone was there, it was already too late—he'd felt the prick of a needle in his neck and it was all over. Blackness, that's all he could remember ... until this. And part of him now wished he was still unconscious.

He closed his eyes, perhaps to pretend, but all he could see were those cuts. Ted could imagine the pain, putting himself in the dead people's places—could feel what he was surely about to experience, when whoever had done this returned.

Ted heard a sound and snapped himself out of his thoughts. A voice. Dear Christ, the killer was coming back already, before he'd even had chance to formulate a plan of action. But no, it wasn't that at all. Someone was speaking, yes, but it wasn't in the assured voice of a murderer. Someone in control of the situation, without compassion—someone who could do the things that had been done in this slaughterhouse.

This was more like a whimper, a groan. "Help me," it said.

Then there was movement. One of the "corpses" nearest to him shifted position, spinning around on the rope that was holding it … her. Because, as Ted could see, this was a woman too; the blouse and skirt, ragged as they were, gave it away. Her face caught the light from the moon and he almost gasped in horror at what had been done to it. Part of the woman's cheek had been ripped away, a large flap of skin peeled off, revealing cheekbone and teeth. The edge of her lip had been torn as well, leaving her with a permanent frown on one side—like a person who'd suffered a severe stroke. No wonder she was having trouble speaking.

Her hair—it appeared silver, but then that was probably just the effect of the light … more probably blonde—looked like it had been hacked at as well: one side cut short, possibly with a knife, while the other was still long and fell over her left shoulder. That too was exposed and horribly scarred. Her head was tilted, and to be honest she still *looked* dead, but she was moving, and she was speaking. "H-Help … Help me," repeated the woman, and this time Ted saw a saliva bubble form in that ruined cheek, popping as she spoke her next word, "P-Please."

What could *he* do? Ted was in no position to help anyone, even if they were gazing at him like that—so pleadingly. It was all he could do to even look at the poor wretch, her appearance so far removed from the usual beauties he liked to associate with. He said nothing, merely attempted a half-hearted shrug.

"*P-Please*," came the voice again, filled with such agony Ted felt compelled to finally say something.

He'd opened his mouth, but before any words could emerge something else moved in the darkness. Something silent and deadly. The something that had come up behind him in the car park, hidden in the shadows all this time. A figure, which sidled up behind *her* now, grabbing the woman's neck and jerking it backwards, so the cords there were standing proud. Ted wanted to look away, but it all happened so fast. The large knife was suddenly up and being drawn over the woman's throat, like a cellist with a bow. Except the only music that emerged were the deep grunts and chokes of someone trying to breathe. A concerto in death minor. It took just moments for the noise to stop, but seemed like hours to Ted—must have seemed like *years* to the woman with the ruined face.

The figure still held back behind the hanging body, for now it *was* a body and nothing more. That final bit of life had been extinguished, such as it was. Ted wanted to ask who this person had been, but couldn't get a word out now through fear. Blood was pouring from the slit in the blonde woman's throat, spilling over her shredded blouse. Ted caught a flash of eyes looking at him, the killer's wild stare sending chills through his body. When the figure revealed itself, he did gasp.

Audrey? No, it couldn't be!

Ted took in the sight before him, the small woman dressed in dark clothes, almost like she was in mourning: black top, black trousers ... black *gloves*. It matched her raven-coloured hair, which, unlike the dead blonde woman's, had been styled by a professional. Even after all that excitement there was barely a curl out of place, the mark of an expert hairdresser. An expensive one, at that.

Ted could do nothing but gaze at her, that knife still in her hand, dripping with the blood from her fresh kill. Audrey? *His* Audrey. She was no murderer. She wouldn't even let him kill spiders in the bath.

His mind flashed back to their first meeting, at that club in the city. She'd been with a couple of friends, he'd been alone and had zeroed in on her, flashing that confident, charming smile, guaranteed to work. Her friends had giggled at his jokes, Audrey had told him she wasn't interested, that she even had a boyfriend—he hadn't lasted long once Ted was on the scene— but by the end of the night he'd secured her phone number.

On their first date, he'd picked her up in his Corvette ZR1 and impressed her with talk about his business ventures. He found out that she was very family orientated—devoted to her father, because he'd brought her up when her mother had died in childbirth.

"I feel so comfortable telling you all this," Audrey had said. "Don't know why."

"I do," Ted replied, grinning.

It hadn't been long before he'd become a permanent fixture in her life ... and her bed. Soon after, they were dividing their time between his place and her apartment. Not long after that, she'd taken Ted to meet her father, Frank, at the family home—a huge house just outside the capital. It was far enough away to pretend it was the countryside, but just close enough to smell the exhaust fumes from the cars. Here Frank lived, all alone—retired due to ill health, but content. Ted had done the same with her silver-haired father, charming him as they drank wine in the garden, finding out more about the family business.

Frank had made his money through scrap over the past few decades, but the trade went back a long way. "I can remember doing the rounds with my dad as a kid, collecting all kinds of stuff in a horse-drawn cart on the streets, ringing the bell. Nowadays it's all in trucks and vans," he said, laughing. "You know, a lot of people think that Rag and Bone men only go back a couple of hundred years, but some say it's further. To the middle ages, or maybe even before that."

"That's fascinating," Ted told him, stifling the yawn that was building.

"They got their name because they'd even collect rags, which could be sold to paper-makers and weavers, and the bones from meat. That could be turned into bone char, bone ash, bone carver ... even glue!"

Ted listened, humoured the man, but he didn't care about *how* Frank had come by his cash—the heritage obviously important to this guy. He was only interested in the fact that Audrey would come by it one day. Less than a week later, and with Frank's approval, Ted proposed and was delighted when Audrey said yes. They were happy, both of them, and went on that way for a good year or more—

So why was she doing this? He felt like asking her, then hesitated, still seeing that crazed look in her eyes. Something had changed. She was no longer the woman he knew as his fiancée. She was something else—something *unhinged*.

His eyes were at least adjusting to the light better, and he could see more of his surroundings. More of the corpses that filled this place, although he still didn't recognise it.

"There, that's better," Audrey said, stepping away from the dead woman, her voice cold and hard. "Another one of your whores silenced."

Ted frowned. What was she talking about? His eyes flitted from the psychopathic Audrey to the dead woman. Did he know her? Forget about the scarred face and body, the blood; take all that away and did she look familiar? Ted still couldn't see it. He looked around at the other bodies nearby, and beyond Audrey. Yes, they were *all* female, he could see that. But—

Another one of your whores …

He tried to swallow, but was having difficulty. He'd never known their names, any of them, but yes, the more he looked, the more his eyes adjusted to the light in here … *Jesus*, he said to himself. He thought he'd been so careful.

It stood to reason, no one woman was ever going to satisfy *him*. That wasn't how he was made. He loved Audrey, in his own way, and the others were just conquests—to keep his hand in. Sex, nothing more. Plus which, they all knew he was engaged: he'd told them and they hadn't seemed to mind. If anything, some of them found this a turn on.

The more he focused, forcing himself to see the walls of that room, the more he could make out the evidence of those encounters he couldn't resist. No, that made it sound like they'd seduced him, when it was so obviously the other way around. All those nights working late, at conferences or attending business meetings, when actually he was on the prowl again, on the hunt. The photos were there, tacked up on those walls: large, grainy, black and white prints. Some of him and women at bars, at hotels, at clubs like the one where he met Audrey. Some were even worse. Snapshots of the hot, frenzied couplings, rutting like animals—through windows, and some from inside the room itself (a professional then, some kind of P.I. … so Audrey hadn't been as naïve as he thought; it explained why she'd stalled over the wedding). Ted looked from the pictures of those women alive, to the dead bodies hanging in that basement lair. And, God help him, he was able to match them up. Well, most of them. Some were beyond even his identification.

Ted could imagine the pain Audrey had felt when she'd seen some of those photographs. Pain that might tip you over the edge. Pain he now saw in her look—along with revenge. She'd been on her very own hunting trip and now that she'd punished the women who'd slept with him, Ted was next. What was the betting she'd saved the most brutal tortures for last?

He was about to plead with her, but knew that would do no good. Once Audrey had made her mind up about something, that was it. But as she approached, still wielding the knife, he found himself whimpering, "Please, *no*."

When she continued on anyway, he gritted his teeth, the real Ted emerging. "You'll never get away with this, Audrey. I'm telling you. What the fuck do you think you're going to do with all these bodies anyway?"

She paused, as if contemplating this—maybe the first time she'd even considered it during this whole spree. But Ted should have known better. Just as she'd been clever enough to hire the snoop, she'd had her endgame figured out well in advance. Audrey leaned in, too quick for him to flinch, and whispered, "He knows what you've done, and he's coming for you."

What? What the fuck did that mean? Ted braced himself for Audrey to strike, to begin slashing him with the knife. But she didn't. Instead she pulled back, grinning (it reminded him of his grin, that—the satisfied one he couldn't help whenever he'd scored). She was stepping away, leaving him alone. *Don't question it*, he told himself, *it at least buys you some time*.

Then he heard the sound. At first it seemed a long way off, that bell. Then the call followed it, equally distant. "*Rag and Bone!*" it went.

Ted cocked an ear. There it came again. The bell, and the cry: "*Rag and Bone!*"

Audrey's grin widened and she moved over to the side of the room, climbing some steps. At first Ted thought she might be ascending to an upper floor, but then she reached above her and undid a latch. Audrey flung open the doors—cellar doors that led to the outside.

His first thoughts were: I can use that to escape, if only I can get free of these bloody ropes. His next thoughts, when the light from the moon illuminated more of that place, were about those wine bottles at the back of the cellar. Ted knew where he was now, even though he'd never been down here. Had only been to the place itself on a handful of occasions. It was the wine cellar in the family house: a hobby of Frank's and perfect for something like this. No-one would hear the screams. And they were far enough away from civilisation that nobody would hear the cry drawing closer and closer, louder and louder.

"*Rag and Bone!*"

It was a strange call, like the person shouting it couldn't quite say the words. It reminded Ted of how newspaper sellers on street corners shout out the names of the tabloids.

"Audrey," Ted began, but she was taking no notice. She was too busy looking out through the trap door. Ted heard the sound of hooves next, accompanying the bell and the cries.

Jesus, what was going on here? One of her dad's old mates drafted in to help? It made sense. Like Audrey, they really wouldn't have been too happy if they knew the truth.

"*He knows what you've done, and he's coming for you.*"

But what had he done, really? All Ted had suggested was that Audrey invest in a few of his ventures—she had the money now, and it would really help him out (his flashy cars and dinners a front for covering how badly he'd got into debt). Selling the family business wasn't asking too much, was it? Her father had been the one hanging on to the past, why should she?

So she'd done it, even though she was doing other things behind his back (he could talk), hiring that P.I. for example. Audrey had sold up because she loved him.

The scrap business scrapped, Ted bailed out.

He saw the horse's feet now, pulling up outside, the cart behind. And from this angle, Ted could also see the boots when they jumped down—big, hobnailed ones, crunching the gravel around the back of the house. A faint whistle drifted down into the cellar, echoing throughout.

Audrey pulled back, waving a hand and inviting the newcomer

in. The larger figure descended. Bulky, wearing some kind of long coat, he also sported a cap that was pulled down low on his head. His frame virtually blocked out any light from above, leaving the figure in silhouette as he glanced at Audrey—awaiting orders, it seemed. She pointed to the bodies and the man nodded, stomping over to the first. He hefted it onto his shoulder like it weighed nothing, whistling happily.

So that *was the plan?* thought Ted. *Get this bastard to dispose of the evidence of Audrey's sick and twisted exploits?* He said nothing as, one by one, the corpses were carried up the steps and—though he couldn't see properly—he assumed, dumped into whatever cart was up there. Why a cart, he had no idea. Why not a van or truck? Was he some kind of purist or something? Not even Frank had been that bad.

Frank ... Ted thought about the old man now, and about what he'd done.

He shook his head; there wasn't time for that. He was in *real* trouble. As the last of the women were carried and loaded up, Audrey pointed towards Ted. She obviously couldn't bring herself to do anything to her lover. Instead, she'd shown him what she'd done to his "whores" and was now leaving Ted to the attentions of this nutter. He didn't know which was worse. At least he might stand a chance of talking Audrey round. Possibly. Maybe.

But there was no chance of that now, because the collector was next to him, whistling, shouldering Ted and cutting the rope attached to the ceiling. Ted groaned as he was given the fireman's lift, the rotten stench of the man like garbage. It was only when he was being carried that Ted noticed the shabby clothes the guy was wearing, the state of the coat not dissimilar to the dress of Audrey's victims; trousers scuffed and tatty.

Then Ted was being hauled up into the night air. He tried to struggle, but again it was either the position he'd been in or the after-effects of the drugs that prevented him—he had hardly any strength at all. So, when he was thrown in the back of that cart, an old-fashioned wooden one just like those Frank had described, he couldn't fight back. "Audrey?" he just about managed, as the Rag and Bone man left him, skirting round to the driver's seat at the front.

But Ted's fiancée simply stared after them. Then, as the transportation set off, Ted saw her retreat back down into the cellar—no doubt to clean up—leaving him to his fate.

The ride wasn't a comfortable one. Apart from the stench, some of it from the bodies, most of it from the cart and the man driving it, there were the jolts as it went over rocks or uneven terrain. On one particular bump, Ted found himself rolling over to face a girl who'd had her eyes plucked out, the black sockets staring back at him (what had been her name? Jackie, Debra, Sandra? Who the Hell knew?). He couldn't even muster a scream and was thankful when the next jolt came and righted him again. They seemed to be travelling quite fast though, hardly enough time for Ted to worry about where this guy would be dumping them: burying them in a wood, weighing them down in a lake perhaps? In a deserted quarry?

He was wrong on all counts, because when the cart eventually arrived at its destination, the Rag and Bone Man had returned to his home (one of Audrey's dad's old places perhaps? Had this bloke bought it?). Ted took in the yard when they rode through the gates—a typical scrap merchant's, with bits of old bicycles, worn out beds, washing machines and every other bit of discarded detritus you could imagine piled on every side. It wouldn't be hard to lose a few bodies in that lot. The perfect place, in fact.

The man pulled his horses to a standstill and clambered down. The moon was slipping behind a cloud so Ted still couldn't get a good look at the man's face as he began to unload the contents of his cart. He needed to see him, for when he got away—Ted would need to describe him to the police. Audrey first. Then this guy. The cops would throw the book at them both!

(Oh yes, and what happens when they go digging around in your past? What happens when they find out about Frank?)

The huge figure began picking up the corpses again, putting them over his shoulder. He whistled once more as he worked, which made what he was doing all the more disturbing. He tossed them on the heaps of rubbish as if he was flinging old tyres.

Ted tried to twist away, to get his legs and arms moving, to climb out and get free of this place. Run, find a phone and—

But he was going nowhere. They were down to the last few women in the cart, which didn't take the man long to clear.

"Look ... Hey, I have money," Ted managed. (*Oh yeah, whose?*)

The man ignored him, heaving the last of the scrawny bodies onto a pile of trash.

He turned and began making his way back towards Ted.

"Can't we at least talk about it, please?"

"Help me. P-Please!" The words of that woman back in the cellar rattled around in his head.

The man was drawing nearer. "Please, I don't want to die!" shouted Ted, with more force than he'd been able to muster since he woke.

His captor paused then, lingering as if mulling something over. Then he began to walk off to one side.

Yes! I've got through to him, thought Ted. *Maybe I should offer him some money again?* He frowned, though, as he watched the man rooting around in the rubbish there, fishing something out. As the large figure turned, Ted saw he was holding up a cracked mirror.

And, as the guy came back, the moon passed from behind those clouds at the same time as the Rag and Bone Man raised his head. Ted just about had time to register those features—and realise just how appropriate his name was—before the mirror was lifted.

Then it all fell into place. Flashes of the man's face, so similar to Frank's, something he himself had inherited through a bloodline and profession that went back so far. (*A lot of people think that Rag and Bone men only go back a couple of hundred years, but some say it's further. To the middle ages, or maybe even before that ...*) A trade plied during plague times, when they would carry the dead away from infected areas? You don't, you *can't*, do something like that without being granted some kind of immunity by Death himself. They were His helpers, in effect: some even changing to resemble their master.

The rags and bones, all that was left of the dead, were collected by them. By people who were little more than rags and bones themselves. It was a bloodline that had been broken when Ted came along—not simply persuading Audrey to sell up, but engineering the little "accident" that would take Frank's life and provide the means for her to do so. Frank was an old man, his heart weak: it wasn't that hard to sneak inside the house and give him a little ... scare.

Just like Ted was scared now. Because not only was he seeing something he really didn't want to in the mirror, he was also remembering. That it hadn't been the first time he'd woken up back there in the cellar, that Audrey had already done things to him which made the others look like she was just getting started. Pain so intense he'd blocked it out, kept alive—barely—while he watched her cut up the women.

But not kept alive long enough.

The image, the face—or what was left of it—staring back at Ted was barely recognisable as his own. It had been shredded, along with the rest of him: skin flayed from his body so that you couldn't tell where his clothes ended and his flesh began. Ted recalled the whipping now with some kind of cat o' nine tails, spiked ends digging deep with each swipe. He howled then, just as he had when Audrey had done her worst, finally getting up close and personal, pulling off his finger and toe nails, doing hideous things to his privates that meant he'd never be capable of cheating on anyone again.

Ted looked away and the Rag and Bone Man dropped the mirror. His charge had seen enough obviously, but things were only just getting started. Ted looked past the skeletal figure, whose coat could no longer conceal its ribcage, open to the air. This representation of everything Frank held so dear, this figure that was all the Rag and Bone Men there'd ever been rolled into one, had made its home in a fittingly nightmarish place. Because the more Ted looked, the more he saw of the yard, filled not only with ordinary rubbish, but the more specific junk of human waste. Bones, organs, scraps of clothing, all plugged the gaps where he'd dared not look before.

Ironically, Ted felt like laughing. He'd been pleading for his life when all along there was no life to spare. No wonder Audrey had been ignoring him—had he really been speaking at all? Had any of this actually been happening? It certainly felt real to him, but that didn't mean anything.

Somehow Ted knew he would soon fill the spaces here, just like those women who'd wronged Audrey, who'd wrong the line. Trapped in their own private Hell. (For a moment, Ted wondered if they were seeing this, or something else entirely; perhaps this particular treat had been reserved only for him?)

But it was time, he saw. When the Rag and Bone Man came for him now, Ted surrendered without protest.

To be carried over to the pile of junk, of scrap human life.

To join the walls of organs, body parts and muscle.

To join ... no, finally to *become* the rag ...

... and ...

... the bone.

Pay the Piper

He turned intuitively.

Another one lumbered out from behind a dwelling to The Piper's left. He stopped and watched the figure, tracing its path. At this distance it looked tragic, like the town drunkard who remains under the influence long after the taverns have closed. Bottle clutched to his chest, faint mutterings of a song escaping from his lips—or perhaps the laments of a once-happy man.

But as The Piper covered the ground between them, certain truths came to light. Instead of a bottle, the man was holding something that was pink and red and glistening in the early morning sunshine. The remains of his last meal. And in place of a song or words of regret, the sound of burbling wind was emanating from his mouth; half-formed belches released with each step the fellow took.

The Piper stopped now, a few feet from this new suspect. It looked up at him, no longer an individual in any true sense of the word; one eye glazed over and thick with cataracts, the other hanging down to rest on its cheek, suspended on strips of meaty string—the blood in its empty socket long-since dried up. It took another bite of the forearm clenched in grey, gangrenous hands, one finger bent so far back that it had to be broken; the nails crusted and black as if it had been digging for coal.

It chewed the meat in an unconscious way. This was merely a habit, something it felt it must do. There was no reason for it to eat anything at all; its digestive system was no longer in any fit state to process food and it was hardly likely to keel over and die from lack of sustenance. You could only die once. That was accepted, a fact of life. One of the rules of creation.

One of them.

As it worked the muscle and bone around inside its mouth, grinding the portion down until it felt able to swallow, it stumbled forwards. The rags it wore flapped behind in the mild breeze, but here and there pieces of its skin were exposed and The Piper looked upon the foul grubs and insects that had made their nests in its rotting body. Bits of earth still fell from its breeches when it "walked", gathering around its bare feet, waiting to be trampled back into the land once more.

The Piper often wondered what went through their minds, if, indeed, such uncanny vagrants even had minds. Were their souls somewhere else, on another level exploring magnificent territories beyond his ken, detached from these ungainly vessels they once inhabited in life? Or was there still some small fragment of humanity lurking inside each one, trapped in there and screaming for deliverance? Trying to prevent themselves from committing such unholy acts because if they didn't, they would never reach the great hereafter and sit with The Lord and his angels and ...

The Piper shook his head. He knew full well what this repellent wretch was thinking about. It looked at The Piper—as best it could, given the circumstances—and saw another succulent dinner ready prepared. It did not, by any stretch of the imagination, see a person standing there. Just food, and plenty of it; enough to last a good few hours, starting with that nice juicy brain inside his skull. This was always the first to go for some reason. He'd noticed that. He'd noticed many things in his time.

But The Piper had no intentions of being devoured. Not today.

He showed not a flicker of fear as he reached for the instrument tucked into his belt, a long wooden tube with holes down the middle and a flattened out mouthpiece. The work of a true craftsman. His own work, in fact. The dead thing had now dropped its snack and was "speeding" towards the main course. Those shaking hands stretched out, flashes of bone poking through at the knuckles, worms hanging down off the wrists like living, squirming bracelets.

There was now only a gap of inches separating them and a putrid aroma filled this modest cavity. It was just about to grab

The Piper's arm—and a second later force him to his knees—when the first note was played. The carcass stood paralysed as the gentle sound carried past its ears, or what was left of them. A second note followed, then a third and a fourth, until a melodic tune took shape. A combination of vibration and breath jetted out of the pipe's end like a sort of magic current. Someone had even told him once that they'd seen shapes and symbols flowing from the whistle—musical notes of differing size and colour. The Piper didn't actually believe this himself (in all honesty he put the man's visions down to either terror or one sip too many of some intoxicating brew or another), but such stories could do nothing other than bolster his soaring reputation.

The Piper's long, bejewelled fingers gambolled over the holes as he blew. Slowly, the thing that had once been a living being, backed away. Its arms fell to its side, bewildered by its own actions. And ... aye, a slight smile appeared on its face. Its cracked lips parted, pulled back over browny-black teeth. This was more like it.

Without further ado, The Piper turned his back on his captive audience and started walking again. It would follow him, they always did. Even now, above the noise of his pipe, he heard the shuffling behind: the empty croaking. It wasn't something that could be fought or questioned.

When he played, they obeyed.

All his life he'd known he had a purpose, a destiny. That he was somehow different. But for most of his childhood he'd been wilful and directionless, finally cast out by his adoptive family because they couldn't cope (his true origins still remained a mystery; abandoned in a basket in the Village Square). Training as a 'prentice carpenter had seemed like the answer for him, a discipline and direction he lacked at that time.

Old Jed had been his mentor when no one else would take him in. He'd taught him how to respect and manage the wood, to fashion it into any object he wished, from tables to chairs and even playthings for the young. He'd enjoyed his studies, but still longed for something more. Something special to happen. An objective, and maybe even riches beyond his wildest imaginings ...

He used to watch the noblemen, traders and travelling merchants who would oft-times pass through the settlement, wishing he could be just like them. To explore the provinces, and further afield than that, must truly be an amazing thing, he thought. They told stories of distant lands where a man was sure to make his fortune, and a different maiden would warm his bed each night. Jed had laughed and called him a dreamer. In a sense he was just that. He would never live the fantasy life he'd mapped out for himself, never in a million years. Or so he had thought. That was before ...

This was now.

The Piper led his new recruit through the streets of the town. At windows he saw the frightened inhabitants pointing, talking of him.

"There goes The Piper," they would say. "Listen to his music."

Children idolised him. They dreamed their own dreams of one day becoming just like the man in the splendid tunic and single-feathered hat. But he was providing an essential service for the adults as well, without which they would not dare set foot outside in the light—never mind the darkness hours—for fear of running into one of the ground-dwellers.

(This was the name they had acquired over the years. It made them sound more ... human than they were. Not something that couldn't be understood or reasoned with. The Piper had never approved of the label himself, which likened them to some exotic new subterranean race who, jealous of the life above, had suddenly decided to come up and say hello. Why couldn't people just face the truth? These were—or had been—brothers, sisters, parents, cousins, friends ... folk they had buried but refused to stay that way.)

The Piper remembered how his own community had been the first time, how they had reacted to this unheard of occurrence. The disbelief and ignorance.

One story in particular had remained with him, that of a young girl he'd known and admired (from a distance, alas). However, on this Sunday aft her family and betrothed had been consigning her to the grave, mere seconds away from placing her in the freshly dug orifice. And all the mourners were especially alarmed to hear the woman knocking inside her casket, needing to be set free.

Now, in spite of the fact that the people there present were conversant with how she had met her end—attacked and beaten on the way home from market—they convinced themselves that by some divine miracle she was still alive. Her beau ran to the wooden box (a box, incidentally, The Piper had helped to make; sobbing as he worked), urging those round about to prise open its lid. The banging came louder and more frenzied. She wanted to be with her loved ones again, and he, being a devoted, caring swain, wished the same. All those lonely days since she went away, all the tears he'd shed, enough to fill a small lake, were forgotten. It had simply been a nightmare which had now relinquished its hold.

But the true nightmare was yet to come.

As the cover was wrenched off, the man had fallen gratefully into his beloved's extended—if disjointed—arms, hugging her tightly, kissing her cheeks, her lips, her forehead; every available patch of skin.

Bystanders looked on, puzzled, as the girl went to do the same. Had she simply been rendered unconscious by the ordeal? they asked one another. Had the local healer been hasty when he declared the lass to be dead? Quite obviously she was not deceased, the way she was embracing her love like that. Oh mercy, another few minutes and she would have been six feet under. A dead 'un alive.

How apt that last description had proved, for the *dead 'un alive* was opening her mouth, staring vapidly up at the sky and faces above. But instead of kissing her paramour, her teeth had gnawed their way through the side of his face.

His scream had been muffled, so those who escaped had said; blocked off by the girl's shoulder. The first inclination they had that something was wrong was when he started to kick his feet against the side of the coffin. Then one observer noticed all that blood inside. A horrible display to be sure.

But there were more to come, as barely recognisable hands broke through the sacred soil of the churchyard. Remnants of locals once fondly remembered were climbing out of their "final" resting places and attacking the guests at this rather premature funeral. Soon the place was filled with the unsteady hordes; some almost skeletal, they'd been horizontal for so long; all hungry for those who still enjoyed the benefits of breathing.

Most fled from the ground-dwellers as fast as their legs could carry them. But some did not make it. The elderly, the infirm, those frozen with fright, all overwhelmed by sheer numbers.

The strong, young men of the village, those who had not yet been drafted into service but bragged about their fighting prowess to all who would listen (aye, and laughed at The Piper because of his scarecrow-like frame), came out to oppose the withered masses before they progressed too far into the settlement—where people hid in their houses and prayed for salvation. The bang of gunpowder and swish of swords could be heard all round, but in the end it did no good.

An arm here, a leg there. The outcome was never in any doubt. How could they possibly kill that which had already expired? The very utmost all these warriors could manage was to slow them down before they too joined the ground-dwellers in death, some as rations, others as converts to their tacit cause.

And this is how it went on. In village after village, town after town, they sprang up, one following the next. With no explanation, no reason. The more superstitious said it was a curse on the land, witchcraft and sorcery afoot. The rational thinkers banded together and stated that it was some strange malady, one which placed its victims in a deathly state then reanimated them after a certain amount of time had passed (but why then was the time period different in each case? critics argued. Some ground-dwellers had been interred many, many years ago, while others, like the woman at the funeral, had barely started to turn cold). No one could offer any real solutions; no one understood what was happening. But perhaps no one was meant to ...

There was a shrill cry from up ahead and The Piper ceased his playing. The ground-dweller halted also. When he saw who was calling out for help, he began running across the town centre, leaving the corpse where it was. It wouldn't attempt to move now; it would simply wait there patiently for his return—the stony grin breaking upon its face.

The Piper could see what the trouble was. Someone had disregarded his express instructions and dared to step out. A lad of no more than fifteen was being dragged across the dirt by his hair. The ground-dweller was female this time, a woman who had probably been sturdy in life, but was now like a deflated pig's bladder: the pleats of flesh dripping from her, dry cuts all over her face and arms where she'd swum her way through wood and packed turf in her hurry to reach daylight. It never ceased to amaze him how they could do that; how strong they could be if they set their sights on something. Why, before now he'd even seen them turn over carts and punch through solid rock to get to their victims.

The boy was yelping as the ground raked his backside. The dead woman was hauling him off to a place only she could see, a place where young, tender striplings were for dining on only.

The Piper positioned himself in front of her, avoiding her free arm as she swung it at him. Great clumps of hair had fallen out, he observed, and that same glassy expression possessed her, the one they all wore. Until, that is, he started to play again, concentrating intently on what he was doing. Then it was quite a different tale.

She let go of the boy and cackled peaceably to herself, almost as though she'd been expecting this to happen.

As he led her off to join her own kind, he heard the bleating youngster shout out after his mother. A mother who had died a good year or so ago, by the look of her. The Piper understood now why he'd broken cover, if only to see his late ma again one final time; The Piper had never known his own mother, abandoned as he'd been, but he could appreciate what drove the youth. Except this was no longer the loving parent he'd known, as he found out to his cost. The Piper felt a trace of emotion and anguish for the deluded boy. Told that his mother was gone, only to witness her walking as large as life—as death?—down the street. Then the empathy disappeared. The Piper picked up the other ground-dweller and they were on their way again. Stumbling behind him, they resembled touched lunatics. But never did he look back once; for if he had he might have seen the boy again, the boy who was so familiar. A mirror image of himself at that age. Before ...

Before his name had been known far and wide? Just a carpenter's'prentice with a big mouth and even bigger aspirations. That would all change soon enough, though. As soon as he discovered his secret, his latent ability. Something no one else in the world could lay claim to.

Aye, he had been a face in the crowd who hid when the ground-dwellers stormed their village that first time, fresh from the funeral. Covering his eyes as the mayhem outside his workshop gathered strength. The dead like a festering wave sweeping into the alleys, trying to break into houses. Old Jed had seen the things take those young 'uns, had seen how easily they'd swallowed them up ... in some cases quite literally. But still he insisted on going out to face them, armed only with his few craftsman's tools. He ignored the teenage Piper's pleas, his half-mumbled explanations.

"I won't just sit here and watch 'em take the village, son."

Those were his last words, unless you count the pitiful screams as he vanished beneath a swell of decaying forms, his bones picked clean in a matter of minutes.

If only there was something I could do, The Piper had thought. But he couldn't control them. This was beyond the wisdom of his years. It was only when they burst into the workshop itself, splintering doors and smashing up tables, that he discovered there was something he could do. There was plenty he could do (if only he'd realised it sooner ...). Instinctively, as the first of them drew near, its chin hanging off on a piece of gristle, the cheekbones dirty-white where they split skin as crumbly as dried parchment, he became aware that actually he could control them, could master this new power rushing through his veins. He just needed to channel it somehow ...

But he was also scared, overcome by the forces unleashed upon his home. So terrified that he scrabbled around on a nearby bench for a weapon in case he should falter. And his fingers, those long, artistic fingers, had closed around the pipe: a child's trinket he had been making all that week. As yet it remained untreated, the wood still naked and cream; hardly resembling the shiny brown object he now carried about with him everywhere.

But something told him to play.

And to his surprise the devils curtailed their advancement into the workshop. More than that, they all fell back—about eight in total, including the girl from the funeral—smirking and bobbing their heads to his tune. A tune he played confidently, though he'd never picked up a whistle in his entire life before now, only to plane and chisel at one.

The ground-dwellers parted and allowed him safe passage outside, where he discovered his music had the same soothing effect. Of course, he knew that it wasn't the flute or the music alone that was doing this, but rather his own persuasive knack. The pipe merely allowed him to direct the energy from within. He couldn't explain it. It was just so. However, the villagers didn't know this. They believed it was The Piper's harmonious notes that kept the savages at bay. And as he strode out to the edge of the village, the ground-dwellers fighting to keep up, he became a legend—his old family being the very first to offer praise. How did he do it? No one knew ... including The Piper himself! No one cared. He had saved them all and was amply rewarded for doing so.

Thus began his travels. The fulfilment of his dreams. Dressed in an outfit more suitable for his purposes, the pointed hat with a feather stuck in it a finishing touch (the people expected no less of their heroes), he visited "infected" towns and hamlets, ridding them of the ground-dwellers in exchange for a few nights' board and lodging. That and a modest payment. Well, modest compared to losing their lives, he argued. And most folk agreed. They were happy enough to oblige. Nobody could offer the same service as him, at least nobody he had ever come across, leaving the field wide open for him to set out his stall.

He'd earned prodigious sums of money during his time abroad this land, had met so many people—some good, some bad—and his myth had grown in proportion to his remarkable feats. One day, he'd decided, when the scourge was over, he would retire and live like a king. But for now there was still work to be done.

The Piper led his two prizes through the streets. He resisted the urge to dance to his own rhythm, although he had been known to do so on occasion in other locales, where the inhabitants cheered him on from the windows. There was no such outward encouragement from these people.

He made another sweep of the town to pick up any stragglers he may have missed on the first few rounds. The Piper found two more to add to his collection, then took them to the boundary where he had deposited his earlier hostages. He looked out over the assembly of around forty ground-dwellers, each one decomposing at a different rate. They gaped back at him, wondering what he would do with them.

The Piper had an idea they already knew. They had been on their little excursion, enjoyed the freedom while it lasted, but would be glad to return to the only homes they recognised now. He played his tune louder, steering them back. It must have been an eccentric sight, the carrion procession marching on like that. Though no less astonishing than the sight of them coming over the hill in the first place. The Piper arriving some time later to save the day once more. Payment had then been swiftly negotiated with the town's spokesman, a sly-looking man by the name of Halberry. Could he be trusted? The Piper hoped so.

Now the graveyard wasn't far away, and it didn't take long for the corpses to find their respective plots. The Piper directed the operation, urging them to settle back into holes that they'd made themselves. One by one they pulled the sod back over, like a sleeper pulling blankets up over their head. Bedding down; asleep once more.

The Piper took the whistle from his mouth, another job finished. As he walked back down the town's path, he meditated silently. Would these folk pay as they had promised? Sometimes, when they saw the ground-dwellers were gone, people foolishly believed they didn't need his services anymore. Why should they compensate The Piper now that the crisis was over? He prayed they wouldn't take that attitude. They seemed like fairly nice people (an image of the boy flashed through his mind). He would hate to see what happened in the last town happen here again. Today.

But if for some reason they did decide to renege on the deal, he would just have to persuade them. It seemed to be what he was best at, persuasion. Of the living and the dead.

No, if they refused to pay The Piper it would not bode well for the population of this town. He might be forced to undo all his crucial work, a waste of everyone's time and effort. However, The Piper would have no choice but to make another example of them, calling the dead to rise just as he'd seduced them back to their mounds.

After all, had he not raised them up in the first place? Raised them all up in his time. In village after village, town after town ...

And if this were true, if he really was The Piper, what on God's green Earth was there to stop him from doing so again?

Thicker Than Water

Meeting the family, it was a big step: a watershed.

Was there any wonder Naomi was getting cold feet now? Was getting jittery, in spite of the fact it had been her who'd insisted they should make this trip? That it was about time, after almost eight months of seeing Gerry? Only now the day was here, she wasn't so sure. What if they didn't like her? What if they hated her, in point of fact? Thought she was no good for him? Couldn't stand the idea of her being with their Gerry? Couldn't stand the sight of her?

Calm down, Naomi told herself. *Look at the scenery and relax for Heaven's sake!* And it was beautiful, it had to be said: all greens and yellows, rolling by the passenger window of the car as they drove along idyllic country lanes. In a year which had seen one of the harshest winters this country could remember (followed by devastating floods in its wake), Spring had finally arrived—indeed, it was so late it was almost giving way to the summer months.

She always did this, Naomi reminded herself when she found she still couldn't settle. Built things up, imagined the worst-case scenario. Whatever could go wrong, would. Claimed she wasn't a pessimist, but rather a realist (painfully aware of the irony that every single pessimist in history had said the same). Couldn't allow herself to think things might work out, that she might well be happy this time, because of all the crap she'd been through before. All the heartache ...

The abandonment.

Naomi shook her head. No, not today. She wouldn't allow it. Those dark thoughts could just go away, like dark clouds chased off by the sun. No rain, no storms today ... or at least she hoped not.

It wasn't something she was used to doing, if she was honest: hoping. Not anymore, not these days. Well, not until Gerry came along anyway. Hadn't started out that way, she'd been quite a hopeful child she thought, always looking to the future but enjoying the present. However, losing both parents in quick succession at an early age—one to a debilitating disease and the other to suicide, she was told—tended to shake your confidence in the world. Destabilise you. A series of orphanages and foster carers later (no real homes, no real families) and she was out there being battered by the cold, harsh reality of the world; always the quiet one at university, then at work. The outsider. Never getting into the madness that was around her: the nightclubs, the drink and drugs ... the casual sex.

Naomi told herself it was because she was better than that, she had more respect for herself than to get into the whole "one night stand" or "try before you buy" thing. And there was an element of that involved; *of course* there was. Saving herself, they used to call it. But she was also scared. Scared of the consequences of letting go, of losing herself, of opening up—opening her *heart*— to someone.

There had been boys, naturally. Someone who looked like she did was bound to get hit on (a natural beauty, apparently), and there were some she'd genuinely liked—those she thought liked her back for who she was. But when it came right down to it, none of them had waited until she was ready to *be* with them; to give herself to them. And the few times she had been stupid enough to almost—

Let's just say she'd learned her lesson, but good. Life wasn't a fucking Disney movie. You put your trust in people, they invariably let you down, deserted you.

Until she'd found Gerry.

She looked across at him now, sitting there in the driving seat of his sporty silver BMW, shifting gears as they crested a hill, and Naomi couldn't help smiling. He'd been good for her, Gerry. Was perfect for her. Naomi's smile faded at the thought of that word. Nobody was perfect, let alone someone who might be interested in her ...

Might be interested? He adores *you, you idiot!*

Still, nobody was perfect ... but he was just so, so ... perfect! She couldn't think of another word that adequately described him. The fine blond hair, which matched his eyebrows. Perfect cheekbones, pouting lips any male model would think themselves lucky to be blessed with, such penetrating eyes. And that body of his ...

It had been the first thing she'd seen of him. Sleek and lean, yet well-muscled, he was the only thing Naomi had noticed as she'd walked out through the back doors of the hotel at the tail end of last summer; part of the holiday she'd promised herself and saved up for after another miserable few months.

In front of her was the pool she'd been intending to read and sunbathe beside—though she was hardly likely to get a tan when she was mostly covered by that sarong and floppy hat. But absolutely no swimming, she hated getting wet ... or was it just the stripping off to a bathing suit? Anyway, when she looked up, she'd been expecting to see the usual gaggle of children messing about, the older folk splashing around as they did their lengths for exercise. But instead she'd seen *him*, Gerry, gliding through the water arm over arm, as fluid as the liquid he was immersed in; flesh glistening in the sunlight, making him look as oiled as those strippers she'd witnessed once at a colleague's bachelorette party. But as impressive as those guys had been, they had nothing on Gerry—as she soon saw when he reached the other end of the pool and climbed out.

Realising she was in the way of a couple who were also looking to find a recliner, she'd taken a step—a couple of steps—only to almost trip and stumble. Naomi had never been the most spatially aware of people, never been one to mind her surroundings, but distracted like this ... *Get a grip!* Naomi had told herself. She'd continued on to a seat nearby, trying not to make those glimpses through her sunglasses so obvious. Stealing glances at Gerry (not that she'd known his name then), aware that many of the other ladies present were doing the same. A woman walked past him with breasts that looked like they'd been pumped up at a garage, barely contained in that minuscule bikini top, skin as tanned as leather. But, as she'd taken her seat, Naomi had been impressed and pleasantly surprised by the way he'd hardly noticed that bimbo—continuing to towel himself down after the dip. The woman had walked on by, looking back only once with a frown, clearly not used to being ignored.

Naomi had settled down with her book, looking up a few times to see what the man was doing—sighing when she saw him heading to the bar on the other side of the pool. Resigning herself to the fact that he was probably meeting someone: girlfriend, fiancée, wife. Which seemed to make sense when she saw him with two drinks, two green cocktails with fruit and straws sticking out of the top.

But as amazed as she'd been by his ignorance of the plastic woman, she was even more surprised when he walked over in her direction with those drinks. *Oh no*, she thought, *please don't be one of those cheesy chat-up guys! Don't ruin such a* perfect *fantasy for me, that inside you're something more. That beneath the surface you're—*

Then he'd walked right by her, just like the enhanced woman had done with him, and it had actually physically pained Naomi. She felt that loss so deeply. Worse than finding out he was a dick would be not knowing him at all. So, when he'd skirted around, doubling back and placing one of the cocktails on the table beside her, she let out another sigh—this time of relief. When they talked about this afterwards, Gerry would always say that he'd been aware of her as soon as she appeared—though she knew he couldn't have seen her, he'd been too busy swimming, head in and out of the water as his arms propelled him further away from her. But that was his story and he was sticking to it.

During that first conversation, after he'd asked politely if he could sit on the recliner next to her, she'd found him confident but not overly so. Charming, though not to the point of nausea. But, most importantly, very easy to talk to—and an extremely good listener. He hadn't used any lines, hadn't overly flattered her, he'd simply been Gerry. And Gerry had been lovely.

In the time between their parting and the dinner date they'd arranged for later at a nearby five-star restaurant, she'd wound herself up again, thinking of all the things that might be wrong with him. He was cheating on said girlfriend, fiancée, wife— had kids, a family he wasn't telling her about. He was a rapist, a multiple murderer with a string of convictions to his name ... He worked in the seedy underbelly of the city, pimping out his women to slavering perverts and was going to get her hooked on heroin so she could be next!

All ridiculous, as she'd discovered later. Gerry worked in shipping, imports and exports, above board with legitimate offices, which he offered to show her around (proof enough, she thought to herself, that he had nothing to hide in this department). He negotiated deals, travelled a fair bit—and was also doing very well for himself, thanks (she saw just *how* well with that first piece of jewellery he gave her, a gold necklace—an unusual design, but she liked it). He hadn't needed to save up for the hotel, no siree! Not that any of this mattered to her, she'd never been impressed by wealth; it was simply a bonus that he might be a good provider.

She'd found out then that Gerry had been determined to do well, help out his family who—in a reversal of his fortunes— hadn't been doing so brilliantly of late.

"Only *just* keeping their heads above water, in fact," Gerry had told her sadly after finishing his *salmon en croûte*, staring down into his glass of Perrier as if to further illustrate his statement.

"Oh, I'm ... I'm really sorry to hear that," she'd told him, at the same time envious of this connection he had to them; something she had never really known. Naomi sensed a closeness when he talked about them, his mom and pop, his older brother. His childhood, being taught to fish from the jetty off the side of their house—it sounded idyllic. But she also felt that sadness when he'd had to go out into the world to make ends meet, that he hadn't been able to stay closer to home. In the end, after much deliberation, they'd made his choice for him, insisting he went out there and did them proud.

"You must be happy that you're now in a position to help them out though, surely?" Naomi had said, starting her dessert of chocolate torte, and he'd nodded.

"Yeah, I guess ... " But he'd shaken his head at that point and moved the conversation along, asking her more about herself; her life, her job, her hobbies. "I want to know *everything* about you, Naomi Jackson." His smile spoke of genuine interest. Nobody had ever wanted to know everything about her. Nobody had ever been that bothered. So she'd talked, figuring what did she have to lose?

Hope? She could lose the hope that was starting to build inside of her, the hope that had continued to build all this time. Since she'd found Gerry; since they'd found each other.

Girlfriend, fiancée ... wife? (Family?)

The hope she still had as she sat in the car, travelling towards their destination. But all that could be dashed, everything they'd been through in the last few months could be undone if Gerry's clan didn't take to her. It might change everything, leave everything in ruins. She asked herself again, why had she insisted on this trip? Especially when Gerry had been so uncertain himself.

Maybe she shouldn't have asked him what was wrong when he'd looked so down that day. But Naomi had to know, wanted to make sure it wasn't something she'd done or said. "No, no ... it's just that ... Well, my folks have been in touch and ... Naomi, I hadn't told them about you yet. I just wanted to keep you to myself a bit longer. Now they want to meet you."

She'd be lying if she said she didn't feel hurt by the first bit, but figured she could sort of understand it. All this time together, just the two of them, had been wonderful—the best of her life.

"I didn't want to ... Not till I was absolutely sure about you. About how I felt."

"And?" she'd asked, biting her lip.

He'd looked at her blankly then, questioning.

"How *do* you feel?" she'd clarified.

"Oh ... " He'd smiled then. "That's easy. I worship you, Princess—you know that." The use of his nickname made her melt inside (just like Disney), especially used in that context. "You should do. I've never ... well, I've never felt this way about anyone else."

Anyone else, all the others she'd been instantly jealous of as soon as he'd told her. There had been girls before, were bound to have been, but Gerry promised never anything serious, they hadn't really meant anything to him. Not like this. Now he was with her exclusively—which made her happy. She didn't want to share him with anybody. And it had been his idea to wait, not rush her—though they'd come close a few times, *really* close; her closest yet—because, as Gerry said, they were about more than that.

Never felt this way about anyone else.

Now she just wanted to feel that connection to his family as well, that belonging. Wasn't too much to ask, was it? But, as Gerry had warned her, meeting them would definitely "change things". The next big step (girlfriend, fiancée ... wife; giving her that family), which could go either way.

"It's just that they can be a bit set in their ways," Gerry had informed her again only the other day. "Old fashioned, holding on to the past."

"Anybody would think you don't *want* me to meet them or something?" Naomi had said.

"It's not that, it's ... " Gerry nodded. "Hey, I'm sure they'll love you as much as I do. You're very special, you know."

She'd beamed at that.

But here, now, those doubts—fuelled by Gerry's words—were resurfacing. Worst case scenarios: the mother thought she was a gold-digging whore; the father said they'd disown Gerry if he didn't tell her to get lost; the brother was a monster, was everything she hated in a guy—

No! She willed away the dark thoughts. Easier said than done, when the weather seemed to be turning against her as well. Clear, bright blue skies had now given way to a dull grey horizon with ink-blot clouds that looked like shadows. Even the pretty fields that she'd been staring at in a daze had become strange bog-like stretches of land. When had that happened?

"Enjoy your nap?" asked Gerry.

Naomi didn't even know she'd been asleep. She'd been worrying about what was going to happen when they arrived and then ... Telling herself to relax, she'd obviously relaxed a little *too* much.

Now she'd woken up and everything had taken on a strange dull cast, as if the film of her life had just switched from technicolour to black and white.

"How long was I ... ?"

"Not long. But it's actually not that far now," Gerry informed her. She couldn't tell if he was pleased about that or not. Naomi knew he was looking forward to seeing the brood again, but maybe under different circumstances? Maybe *not* with her in tow. Perhaps they were mad that he'd kept Naomi from them all this time? Moms in particular could be like that, couldn't they? Not that she'd know. Not that she'd ever really known her mom properly before she'd—

(Blood, water. The razor ... How she always pictured it in her head.)

No, stop it. You're doing it again. Stop that right now!

The car carried on, and through the window now she could see the coastline—the angry sea running parallel to them. Rain suddenly started up, striking the windscreen and causing her to jump in her seat.

Battered by cold, hard reality.

"You okay?" asked Gerry, flicking on the wipers, and she gave a small tip of the head.

But she wasn't. Far from it. The downpour was making her even more anxious, doing little to calm her nerves. By the time they were driving down what Gerry called "Federal Street", the rain had settled into a steady drizzle and it was almost dark—in spite of the fact it was only afternoon and the nights were supposed to be getting lighter by the day.

Dark clouds, dark thoughts ... dark place.

Gerry was going to take her on a little guided tour first, he informed her. Naomi wondered if he was just putting off the crunch time, but that was okay—she wasn't in any rush to sink their relationship (she'd already decided in her head by now that this whole thing would be a washout). He pointed out landmarks such as the old churches that surrounded the New Church Green, the hall on her right where the townspeople used to hold gatherings, the old town square and what had once been the refinery, before they passed over the bridge which ran across the Manuxet River and he drew her attention to the lighthouse in the distance. When he spoke about his hometown, it was with such a sense of pride, of belonging, and Naomi wished that she could experience that as well. Because all she saw was a place that might well have been really nice once, but was now in a state of disrepair and ruin.

Everything in ruins ...

Gerry was clearly seeing all of this through rose-tinted glasses; as if through the eyes of a child. And that smell! Naomi did her best not to crinkle up her nose, but the aroma was so strong. A distinctive stench of the ocean, of fish.

Touring round the town square, Gerry showed her the old fire station, the Gilman House hotel, a couple of stores and what had been his favourite restaurant when he'd lived here. "Makes the best calamari in the northeast," Gerry stated; he did so love his seafood. It looked like a bit of a dive to Naomi, but she said nothing.

Gerry's family lived down by the sea itself, she knew, and Naomi peered over when he pointed to exactly where. It looked like some of the worst houses were situated down there, their wood and brickwork plagued by rot. He hadn't been kidding when he said they were barely keeping their heads above water ... in every respect. She couldn't help gaping across at him then.

"Your parents ... live down *there?*"

"Ahuh," he said simply.

She looked again, thinking maybe she was missing something— but she wasn't. If anything this closer scrutiny showed her that the problem was even more severe; some of the houses were tilting, as if they were about to simply fall into the waves and be swept away.

I know Gerry said they weren't doing brilliantly, but this is ridiculous, thought Naomi. All that money he earned, how little of it must he have been sending back home for them to still be living in such squalor? In such a town as this?

A ghost town, for in all the time they'd been driving around, Naomi had yet to spot one person. Yes, it was raining and she didn't blame anyone for staying indoors in such poor weather, but that didn't explain why the buildings all looked deserted as well. There were no lights on, nothing. It was almost as if they wanted to purposefully give the impression here that nobody was home.

She was about to mention this to Gerry when he suddenly turned and said, "I guess we'd better be heading off to see them then."

Naomi nodded slowly, feeling her guts tying themselves into knots. Gerry steered the BMW down a couple more streets, then parked it up by the side of the road, telling her they'd have to walk from there.

"You're kidding?" she said, looking up through the window. It was pouring and she hadn't thought to bring either a coat or an umbrella with her; it had been such lovely weather when they'd set off. Her summer dress would be drenched in seconds. But Gerry didn't appear to be thinking about that, probably more bothered about what his family would think of her—plus it wasn't his fault he couldn't get any closer. In any event, he was out of the car now, slamming the door, so she followed him.

Gerry had his head tilted back, eyes closed. He seemed to be relishing the water on his face, unlike her. She coughed and he finally noticed her, standing there soaking. "Sorry," he said and came round to escort her down the path.

She almost slipped once or twice, especially in those shoes she'd chosen for the occasion—nothing too flashy, but they did have heels. Naomi was grabbing on to Gerry for dear life by the time they arrived at the house: a ramshackle affair that looked like it was on its last legs, with slates missing from the roof. While off to the side was the small jetty Gerry had mentioned: uneven and held up by posts, it dipped and tilted and apparently led nowhere but *into* the sea itself.

Once again it looked like there was nobody at home.

Naomi got under the cover of the porch, but the rain still wasn't bothering Gerry. Her hair and make-up—which she'd taken so long over—would be pretty much ruined now; so much for first impressions. "Oh Gerry, whatever are they going to think of me?"

"You look wonderful to me," he replied. "Perfect."

Nobody was perfect, especially not her. She must look like a drowned dog.

"It's just a bit of water, they won't mind."

Naomi stared at the battered door. "I'm not so sure this is a good id—" she began, but it was already opening with a creak. Or maybe it was just finally collapsing, hanging there as it was on one hinge. The thought crossed her mind again that Gerry should be sending them more money, either that or relocating them completely. Getting them out of this godforsaken hole.

"Let me go in first," said Gerry, which she had no problem with at all. Then he was gone, swallowed up inside that darkness …

Dark place, dark house …

… and Naomi realised she was standing on the doorstep, what little there was of it, on her own.

Abandoned.

When she did peer inside she saw that there was a light coming from somewhere, flickering and casting shadows. The faint glow of a candle? Maybe there had been a power failure? Or it had been cut off for lack of payment? The putrid paintwork of the place was peeling, or perhaps it was just trying to flee the walls— she knew how it felt. The carpet she was treading on was damp and squishy, but there was little wonder as the rain was finding its way into the house from above. Perhaps that was what had caused the power to go off?

"H-Hello?" she called out, her eyes readjusting to the gloom.

Then she saw them, standing there in the hallway, Gerry next to a woman who was smaller than him, her outline dumpy. Mom-shaped. The dress she had on covered most of her body, made from a thick material. Her hair was tied up in a bun on top of her head, but various strands had leapt out and floated on the air—giving her a look of being submerged. Her smile was warm, though, welcoming. It was her who had the candle, stuck inside some kind of ornate holder.

"Over here," Gerry said, unnecessarily.

Naomi continued to make her way inside, passing a set of what looked like the most rickety of stairs heading to an upper level.

"Mother, this is my ... special friend. Miss Naomi Jackson."

Naomi frowned. She'd been wondering how he would introduce her, when the time came. Is that what she was, then? His friend? You worshipped your *friends*, did you? She was savvy enough to know it was because of the old-fashioned thing, however, the being set in your ways. At least he'd called her special.

But still, *friend?*

The woman stepped forward, stooping, shambling almost in a way that made Naomi want to cover the distance between them to save her the trouble.

"Gerald's teld us so much about yer," said the woman, free hand out.

Naomi shook it tentatively. "Really?"

"Oh yes." Her strange accent made it sound like "yersh". Her eyes twinkled in the light from the candle as she looked Naomi up and down.

"I'm really sorry about ... I must look such a mess," she said to the woman.

"Naw, yer beautiful dear," said Gerry's mother.

That made Naomi smile. "I hate to ask this when I've only just arrived, but I don't suppose there's anywhere I can ... you know, freshen up at all?"

"'Course," said the woman. "Yer've had a long drive." She pointed to the stairs. "Just at the top there, oh and yer'd better take this."

She handed Naomi the candle, which she took with a thanks. Then they went off, leaving her alone again, standing there staring up the stairs she'd have to negotiate. Naomi took her time, very nearly putting her foot through one slat, but eventually she reached the top. The bathroom was opposite, just as Gerry's mom had promised, so she carried the candle through and locked the door behind her.

Water was dripping on her from above, but ironically when she'd placed the candle down and out of its reach, she couldn't get any to come through the taps attached to the chipped sink. The pipes just rattled and gurgled. Naomi sighed when she looked in the cracked mirror in front of her, it was like the Joker staring back. So she picked up a towel in an attempt to dry herself—only to realise that they were just as sopping as she was. Naomi could at least use it to wipe away the worst of the make-up, she told herself.

As she was putting it back on the rail, she found herself gazing across at the old bath in the corner. Her mind went immediately to her own mother, as she pictured her in one very similar, water slopping over the edge as she held up the razor. Drawing it across veins, redness dripping into—

Blood, water. Water, blood.

She shook her head, snatching up the candle again and leaving as quickly as she could. The whole exercise had been a bit of a waste of time really, she looked almost as bad as when she arrived.

Naomi had one foot on the step to come down, when a big splash from the ceiling put out the candle, with no way to relight it. She swallowed, hard—left the candle and its holder on the stairs, as she figured she'd definitely need both hands now. By the time she was halfway down she was on the verge of tears. None of this was going right at all, and to make things worse she could hear raised voices coming from what had to be the lounge—where Gerry and his mom had retreated. She strained to listen, but couldn't tell what the argument was about; all she could make out were male voices, one of them Gerry's.

Though in her heart of hearts Naomi knew it had to be about her. Everything she feared was coming true.

When she reached the bottom and stepped off (a big step) her foot landed in a puddle of some kind. "What the ... " she managed. Instead of just damp, the carpet was now under at least a couple of inches of water.

Naomi swished through this ...

Was there any wonder she was getting cold feet now?

... feeling her way around into the corridor again: aiming for the lounge. The arguing stopped when she reached the doorway and turned the corner. There were a couple more candles in this room, but these were no match for the murk inside. She could just about make out the shapes in there: Gerry with his mom again; and next to her was a seated figure, a man. Naomi squinted, thought that he had no legs at first, then realised he had a blanket over his knees. He was sitting next to a table which had one candle on it, so he was better illuminated than the others.

He was dressed in a suit that looked like it had seen its better days in the previous century—*early* in the previous century. The skin on his face was tight and shiny, as if it was about to rip at any moment, especially at the corners of his down-turned mouth—except for the flesh underneath his eyes, which hung in bags below two white, bulging orbs. He was virtually hairless, didn't even have eyebrows, but then, thought Naomi, what kind of hair could possibly grow on that head anyway?

Gerry's father, had to be.

"Come on in girly, don't be shy," said the man, beckoning with a hand. He sounded like he'd been gargling with those words, before spitting them out. "Let's have a look atch-yer!"

Gerry said nothing.

Naomi ventured in a little further, suddenly all too aware of how her dress was clinging to her, especially when the man's bulbous eyes lingered a little too long on her breasts. What started off as folding her arms across her chest soon turned into a hug she was giving herself, and not just because she was freezing.

"Ahh," gurgled the man. "Preddy you are." He licked his lips; it made Naomi feel physically sick.

"Now, now, Benjamin," said his wife. "Stop that."

No, stop it. You're doing it again. Stop that right now!

"Yer scaring the poor lass."

"N-Not at all," said Naomi, struggling to keep the hitch from her voice.

The woman picked something up from the table with a rattle and a clink. "Would yer like a cup of tea, dear?" she asked Naomi, obviously deciding that the girl was going to get one regardless. "I've just this minute made a pot." Again she was shambling across the space, forcing Naomi to meet her halfway, taking the chipped cup and saucer from her hands.

Naomi looked down at the tea. It was thick and gelatinous ... and, though it was hard to tell, there looked to be a greenish tint to it. The woman was waiting there expectantly. Naomi grimaced, took a sip. It was cold—very cold—and tasted brackish, but she forced it down with another hard swallow. It almost came immediately back up when she saw how the remaining liquid had settled back in the base of the cup, like mud in a river.

"Somethin' to eat, p'haps?"

Naomi thought of the calamari back at the restaurant Gerry had talked about and held up a hand. "Oh, no ... no thank you. I'm really not—"

"So whet d'ya think of our little town then?" This from the father, who practically coughed out the last of his phlegmy question.

"Erm ... it's ... er ... "

"Bin around since the seventeenth century, it has. A hugely successful seaport at one time or annuther."

"It ... " Naomi was struggling for something to say. "Forgive me, but it seems to have fallen on ... dark times of late."

All three of them looked at her, almost in unison—and as if to silently say that they might never, ever forgive her.

"There's bin darker," said Gerry's mother, pulling back to join her son and husband again, wading through the water.

The older folk splashing around ...

"But we endure," her husband added. "We endure. Like as after that nasty business back in the '30s, the persecutions. Some hid, some escaped. But if it hadn't a bin for the War comin' along when it did ... people forgettin'." He shook his head. "We survived those hardships anyway. What few of us were left, we endured."

"Let's not terk about all that," Gerry's mom cut in, trying to change the subject. "Let's terk about yer two. All very excitin', I have t'say."

More than just a friend then, if it was exciting?

"I'm ... That is, Gerry's ... " Naomi began. "You must be very proud of him, all he's achieved."

"Aye," said the mother, "he's a good lad. Loyal, y'know?"

She nodded; Naomi knew that. Everything else aside, all this aside, she was well aware of that. "Proud of how well he's done for himself out there, with his business and everything?"

The man in the chair laughed suddenly then, a sort of strange gurgling noise. "For 'imself?"

"Father," said Gerry. "Please don't."

"You think 'e did all that by 'imself."

"Benjamin!" This was the mother again. "Now's not the time nor the place."

"I'm sorry, but I can't go on pretendin'," said the father. "'im there thinkin' he could just keep her to 'imself like that." He coughed that watery cough again.

Naomi was frowning once more. So they *were* mad about him keeping quiet? Had that been what the argument had been about?

"Thinkin' we'd be all right about the two of 'em!"

No, this was all about her not fitting in again, wasn't it? Just like uni, like work. About her being an outsider, not being accepted. For God's sake, if you couldn't even be accepted here, by these people ... But how would Gerry feel about that, she could see the way he ... worshipped this place. Had basically been forced to leave it so he could try and bail his folks out—the water rising, up to her calves now—but what did his dad mean when he said Gerry hadn't done it on his own?

Naomi was already going through what would happen now in her head. The long drive home in silence, promises to call her when they got back and then never seeing Gerry again. Her ringing and leaving messages on his phone, getting increasingly desperate. Alone, deserted.

No girlfriend, no fiancée, no wife ... no *family*.

Taking the razor, following her mother's lead?

Blood, water ...

She couldn't have been more wrong. Couldn't have thought up this worst-case scenario in a million years.

"Neglectin' his duties, his responsibilities," the father continued on with his rant. And Naomi found she couldn't bite her tongue any longer, no matter how things transpired.

"Gerry is the most caring, responsible man I've ever known!" she blurted out. "I love him—and he loves me. Don't you?"

Gerry remained silent.

"*Caring?*" said his father. "Did yer care about them other lasses yer brought back here, eh? About what happened to 'em?"

All the others, the ones she'd been so jealous of. So they'd been brought back here too? And what had happened with them, he'd dumped them when he got bored? Gerry had told her she was special, that's why she'd wanted his family's approval so much. But now she wasn't so sure, about him or them.

Life wasn't a fucking Disney movie. You put your trust in people, they invariably let you down.

Their relationship was sinking …

"Naomi, it isn't how you think," said Gerry now, finally finding his voice. Making to move towards her, then stopping.

"Aye, you know the way it has to be, boy. I teld yer. You've known all along how this ends, yer were just kiddin' yerself."

"Breedin' or sacrifice," said Gerry sombrely, his tones starting to match his family's.

Pimping out his women … His mother thinking she was a gold-digging whore …

Rapist … multiple murderer …

Yer scaring the poor lass.

"*What?*" shouted Naomi, thinking she'd misheard.

"It's just like I taught 'im, just like fishin'," gargled the father. "'Cept young Gerald's the bait now. We sent him out there, funded him with what was left of the town's gold. He brought back what we needed."

A good provider.

Naomi looked across at Gerry's mom now, and she nodded. "It's true I'm afraid, dear."

Town's gold … Naomi's hand went to her necklace and its symbol.

"Well, we couldn't send out his brother—lookin' the way he does. As natural as thet might be." The father pointed behind her and Naomi turned, screamed when she saw what had risen up out of the water.

Never been one to mind her surroundings …

Devastating floods in its wake …

Blood, water ...

So close she could do nothing *but* see him: the naked thing in front of her. He had the same bulging eyes as the father, but these were much more prominent in the middle of a face that could only be described as hideous, framed by fine, slicked back hair. Lumps and bumps covered the skin, while a set of flapping gills opened and closed on his neck. The mouth was much wider than any normal person's, framed by blubbery lips, and when the "man" parted these he revealed row upon row of needle-like teeth.

Gerry's brother, the monster.

Natural-looking ...

"Came on 'im powerfully quick, it did," Gerry's pop continued. "But it gits us all in the end."

Naomi tried to run past the brother, had to save herself, but he grabbed her, spun her so she was facing the room again— then wrapped two strong arms around her, the webbed fingers gripping.

"Be careful!" shouted Gerry. "Don't hurt her!"

"Yer still don't get it, do you? She's not yours!" snapped Gerry's pop.

"Not *just* yours," corrected Gerry's mother.

Didn't want to share her ...

"Yer ... " She pointed at Naomi. "Yer belong to all o' us. And yet to none o' us. He wasn't lying when he said yer were special, y'know."

"You're all mad!" shrieked Naomi. She was still asleep in the car, hadn't woken up—and this was all some bizarre dream, some nightmare brought on by her fears. Or something in that horrible tea she'd been given? Maybe she'd been poisoned?

"Can't you feel it, child?" the woman asked her. (Inside you're something more ... Beneath the surface you're ...) "It's how yer two found each other, it's why yer felt the way you did."

The connection? Was that what this crazy bitch was talking about?

Was aware of her as soon as she'd appeared.

Always the outsider ...

"Yer blood, dear. It's in yer *blood!* Yer heritage is the same as Gerald's."

Her father's disease? ("Natural as that might be ... ") Her mother not being able to live with the consequences ... ?

Blood in the water ...

Some hid, some escaped.

Escaped and carried on with their lives elsewhere, loving other people, having families, having children ... She'd never known her grandparents, had barely known her parents, but what if—

The woman shambled back over again and held Naomi's necklace up to examine it. "The symbol of The Order. He would be pleased ... *He* will be pleased. The one yer have been saving y'self for all this time."

"What ... what the fuck are you talking about?"

"Yer know. Deep down yer know, child ... Princess."

Girlfriend, fiancée, wife ... family.

Naomi fought against the knowledge, just as she fought against Gerry's brother, but the woman was right. About the blood, about her family. She'd always wanted one and now she'd got it, hadn't she? One who adored her, in fact. It just hadn't been what she'd expected. And she realised then, that she hadn't been abandoned after all.

"A fine catch," burbled the father.

He'd done them proud ...

She was perfect.

The older man's blanket was slipping from his lap and now Naomi could see the many tentacles he had for legs, writhing and sliding over each other. She almost screamed again.

"And thers much to do," said the mother. "A festival t'prepare for, an end of the dark times to look ferward to."

Dark times, dark clouds. Dark shadows ... They had hung over this place for such a long time, and would continue to do so for many years to come. Nothing they ever did would change that, not even giving her to—

A big step ... a watershed ...

She suddenly felt very, very scared: of letting go, of losing herself, of opening up to—

She'd feel the loss so deeply ...

Naomi tried to imagine what would happen to her, the worst-case scenario, but nothing would come. It couldn't, it was beyond her imagination.

All she could see now in her mind's eye was the redness, so thick. Thicker than—

Water ... The water *and* the blood.

The blood and ...

The water.

The Procession

At first he thought it was a fault with the camera. Light being let in through the back. It wasn't a major problem. Indeed, some of his most successful stills had been happy accidents (underexposures, film doubling back over itself inside the camera). But there was something different about these shapes.

Bob Greenan held the glossy paper up to the light. What had once been simply black dots on the negative were now bleached splotches running diagonally along the length of his landscapes. Ill-defined and patchy, they stood in a row on those monochrome hills which were the subject of his pictures.

The first nineteen images had been fine—perfect in fact. Just what Bob had been hoping for. The sun setting on Derbyshire's famous rolling hills, casting shadows over the puff pastry clouds and creating singularly natural chiaroscuro patterns. A photographer's dream.

But as the sun was dragged ever lower and lower, so imperfections had appeared on each shot. A sum of five in total. Bob didn't remember seeing any lights when he'd clicked the shutter those final few times, yet here they were with no explanation other than a possible crack in the camera casing itself.

The photographer examined his Praktica, though for the life of him he couldn't find anything wrong. And anyway, surely that wouldn't cause the light to line up in such a way. Larger on the left-hand side, tailing off the closer to the sun they came. Almost like a queue.

Or a procession.

Puzzled, he pulled on his red bulb again and slipped another negative into the enlarger. The inverted image shone through a filter and, after focusing it, he exposed a new piece of photographic paper for a few seconds. Then he dropped it into the developer tray on his right.

Slowly the scene revealed itself. The same thing again, more white shapes traipsing over the gradient, disappearing into the distance.

Stop bath next, then fixative, and Bob had another enigma ready for inspection. He hung it on his drying line with a clip and scratched his head. Maybe the sun's rays had reflected off the lens somehow. Could that have caused such a pattern to emerge? He doubted it. For one thing the sun had been a dying one, incapable of squeezing that much light out—hence the need for 400 speed film—and for another, any reflections that may have been caught would've appeared randomly all over the place: in the sky, the bottom corners ... not in such an orderly fashion.

Fresh out of ideas, he ambled over to the darkroom door and went back into the cottage proper. He was greeted by a russet blur bounding towards him. Chappie, Bob's energetic red setter, jumped up his legs in a desperate bid for attention.

"Hey boy." He ruffled the dog's coat, avoiding the huge, slobbering tongue lolling out of the side of Chappie's mouth.

Bob sat himself down in front of the TV and flicked it on with the remote. Chappie jumped up onto the couch beside him. The picture wasn't great, but he could see all he needed to. Some man in a jester's outfit was being bombarded with custard pies. He tried another channel: a current affairs programme. And another: a badly-acted soap opera. With a sigh he snapped off the power.

*

It was still relatively early, despite the darkness outside telling him otherwise. He'd been in the cottage all of ten days now and had done nothing but work the whole time. Of course, that was one of the main reasons why he'd bought the property in the first place; so he could escape from the rat race whenever he wanted to and concentrate on his art. For a professional photographer there was nowhere on Earth quite like it. Wildlife, picturesque views, rock formations. The lot. There was enough material here to stage several thousand exhibitions and fill a million hardback books.

But man cannot live on bread alone. Or in Bob's case, sandwiches hastily eaten while scouting for locations or printing up. It was time to get out a bit, meet some of the locals—what few there were—and, more importantly, sample the bitter.

He knew just the place.

*

A short fifteen minute drive down the winding road from the cottage brought Bob to *The Wanderer's Rest*, a pub he'd passed several times before but hadn't visited yet. Until now it had been enough for him to know it was there if he needed it. If the loneliness ever got to him or he felt the desire to interact with something that didn't bark back. His headlights uncovered a flat square of concrete next to the inn. Hardly what you'd call a car park, but big enough for the amount of trade the place received.

Inside, it was just as he'd anticipated. Stone walls with wooden beams and tables, attractive watercolour paintings hanging over the fireplace, and a medium-sized—but adequately stocked— bar. One or two patrons were scattered about the room, quietly enjoying their drinks. Bob felt at home right away.

"What'll it be, sir?" the broad innkeeper said. His cheeks were almost entirely red, and those huge forearms were a testament to many years spent hefting beer barrels and crates around.

"Pint of bitter, please." Bob sat on one of the round stools at the bar, waiting for his drink to be served.

"Not seen you around here before, sir. Just passing through?" asked the man as he placed the frothing liquid on the counter.

"Er, no. I've bought a little cottage up the road a way. The white one over—"

"Aye. I know the one you mean," he interrupted, holding his hand out for Bob to shake. "Why didn't you say so before? First drink's on the house. I'm Abe Fenton, by the way. Owner of *The Wanderer's Rest*."

"Pleased to meet you. Bob Greenan." Bob took a swig of the bitter. It was strong and had real bite, but went down the throat so smoothly it might have been pure honey itself. He let out a grunt of satisfaction.

Abe smiled. "So Bob, what is it you do, then?"

"I'm a photographer, for my sins."

"What, like for a newspaper or something?"

Bob laughed. "No, more artistic than that. Well, I like to think so."

"Ahh, then you've come to the right place for it. Some gorgeous sights round here."

Bob nodded. "I'm working on a series of landscapes at the moment. Trying to capture one particular spot at different points in the day."

"That right?"

"Only there seems to be a problem with my camera or something. Sounds good, doesn't it? A photographer with a broken camera." Bob laughed again and supped some more of the bitter, the pleasant atmosphere relaxing him.

"What's up with it?"

"Not really sure. Some pictures I took up on the hills there came out with white marks on them, sort of going across the frame—"

"When was this, then?" The landlord's face had gone pale and his jaw was twitching.

"Yesterday."

"No, no. I mean what *time* of day." His voice had an impatient edge to it.

"Around sunset. *At sunset*, actually. I wanted to ... " Bob noticed the man was shaking his head. "Why, what's the matter?"

Abe leaned over the bar and motioned for Bob to do the same. "Didn't anyone tell you? I suppose not ... You didn't ought to be hanging around up there so near to nightfall," he whispered.

Bob was intrigued. "Why?"

Abe tapped the side of his nose; Bob was surprised to see that old gesture still in use. "Suffice to say that I don't think them marks on your photos are down to the camera."

For a moment or two Bob wasn't sure what Abe meant. Then the realisation slowly dawned on him. "You can't be serious," Bob chuckled, though he could see the man was earnest enough.

"Think what you like. Only you ain't been here as long as I have. Heard the tales. Some funny things happen on them hills at night. All I'm saying is you should stick to takin' pictures in the daytime, Bob. I'd certainly sleep easier if you did."

Bob felt like laughing again, except he didn't want to offend Abe or his beliefs. Not when he was the proprietor of the only pub for miles. Instead, he thanked him for the warning and promised to be careful in future. Abe seemed to settle for this and was soon back to his jovial, easy-going self. Bob joined in the conversation, said hello to some of the regulars when the landlord introduced them, and even took part in the round of joke-telling that appeared to be a ritual pastime in the pub.

But at the back of his mind was the thought of those lights on the hills, and how he couldn't wait to get out there and take some more pictures.

*

On his return to the cottage, Bob went straight to the darkroom to get his prints.

In Bob's mind Abe was a guy who'd read too many "Unexplained" books and listened to one old folktale more than he should have done. Nevertheless, his warning had fired Bob's imagination. There was an angle here he could use to his advantage (*exploit* was such a nasty word). If indeed something strange was occurring on those hills, and there was bound to be a logical explanation, then it was definitely worth investigating. Who knows, it could lead to his best collection yet. Some of his work might even end up abroad or garner interest in the States.

Excitement was replaced by bewilderment, however, when he plucked his photos off the drying line. Something had changed. He couldn't put his finger on it immediately, then as he looked more intently he saw that the blobs which had been so indistinct before were now slightly sharper in focus. He could see the outlines of figures, actual figures, roaming across the hills. They were still pallid and fuzzy around the edges, but there was no doubt whatsoever: these were human beings walking over the peaks.

Or at least they had been, once.

Quickly Bob hunted for the contact sheet he'd made earlier from his negatives; tiny replicas of the snapshots he'd taken. Reaching for his magnifying glass, he was astounded to find that those last five images had altered as well.

"This is insane," Bob mumbled to himself. Once a print was developed it couldn't just mutate like that. Maybe he'd mixed the chemicals incorrectly in his hurry to get started earlier today, or had bought a dodgy batch of photographic paper with a hole in the light-proof box?

But these assumptions were torn apart soon enough. Even the negatives themselves now had black figures on their plastic surface, proving that it had nothing to do with either paper or chemicals.

Bob had never seen anything like it in all his years in the profession.

A glass of scotch helped calm him down, mixing with the bitter already in his system. Chappie danced around him, staring worriedly up at his master. "You might well look like that, boy. I think I'm cracking up." Perhaps Abe Fenton had been right about the hills. And if he was, then this could be bigger than Bob had first imagined.

All he could do now, though, was to sit on the couch and inspect the pictures again, ignoring as best he could the circumstances surrounding their appearance.

The "people" in his photos all had their backs to him, so he couldn't see any of their faces. They looked for all the world like refugees fleeing a war zone, the kind you see on news reports far too often nowadays. Poor, downtrodden individuals with only a handful of belongings, forced to move out of their homes, their towns, their cities.

The similarity wasn't lost on him. Was this group doing the same thing, running away from some terrible tragedy? If so, what was it? And where were they running *to*? Their destination was just out of sight, over the hill in the distance; or over the next one, or the next ...

Bob couldn't help wondering what had caused the phenomenon. Could this be the site of some past disaster? A battle from the middle ages? A plane crash? He made a mental note to check the libraries in the nearest town as soon as possible.

Bob cast his eye over the forms again. Was he really looking at a reflection of some bygone age? A snapshot? If it was, how come *his* camera had picked it up?

These questions churned around in his mind for hours. Bob would stroll over to the window, peering out into the black night as if expecting to see the procession go hiking past. That way, he could simply ask them ... if he had the nerve.

Eventually the alcohol he'd consumed took hold and Bob dropped off to sleep on the couch, the pictures clutched in his fist, and Chappie sprawled across his lap.

*

His dreams were preoccupied with one subject.

Bob stumbled across the darkening countryside, his feet made of cement. Ahead of him he could see a brilliance, gleaming sporadically. As he came near he realised it wasn't just one light, but rather a succession of incandescent outlines moving deliberately towards the setting sun—which itself boiled and bubbled into a swirling sky.

The photographer struggled to catch them up, absently wondering where his camera was. These scenes were incredible and he had no way of recording them for future inspection. Bob tried to call out after the string of oversized fireflies, but no sound would emerge. *I have to know*, he thought. *Why won't you tell me?*

More and more of the objects were emerging from behind a slit in the landscape. No, not a slit. Bob knew it was the edge of a photograph, its white border unmistakable. He was trapped on the paper with no means of escape. How was that possible? How was any of this possible? The only answers lay in front of him, and Bob urged his body onwards.

Closer, closer, until his fingertips were within inches of the nearest light, turning as it morphed into a recognisable contour.

Bob touched the thing's back. It was freezing. With both hands he tugged at its shoulder in an effort to spin it around. To see—

*

The shrill ring of the telephone shook Bob violently awake. His arms were outstretched, hands grabbing at nothing. He brought one palm back to shield his eyes from the sunlight invading the room.

Beside him on the coffee table, the phone persisted, its headache-inducing wail demanding that he answer. Clumsily, he shifted round and snatched up the receiver.

"Hello? Hello? Bob are you there?" The voice was distant.

"Yeah," he answered, rubbing his eyes.

"Bob, it's Ian." Bob didn't know why he was so surprised. His agent, Ian Swain, was the only person who had his number out here.

"Hi, Ian. What time is it?"

Ian paused, a little thrown by the question. "Er ... It's half eleven."

Shit! I've overslept. "You're joking?" said Bob.

"I never joke about time, Bob. You know that. Time is money and—"

"Money is your god. Yeah, yeah, I remember. What do you want?"

"Just seeing how you're settling in. How the work's coming along."

Bob leaned over and scooped up his pictures, which were now all over the floor. He looked at them for the hundredth time, as if trying to convince himself they were real. The figures were still there. If anything, they were more pronounced than the night before. Bob could even see hands and feet. And were there folds of clothing on the nearest one?

"It's funny you should ask that, Ian, because I'm holding something in my hand right now that'll blow you away."

"Really? *That* good?"

"That good."

Bob heard him whistle down the line. "Well, don't keep me in suspense. What is it?"

"I'd rather you came out here and saw for yourself. I've only got a few at the moment, but I'm going to print up some more this afternoon and I'm off out to shoot again later."

"All right, tomorrow it is then. I'll look forward to it. Anything you need from the civilised world while I'm coming?"

Bob grinned. "That's okay, I think I can manage. See you when I see you."

He replaced the handset. A quick shower, shave, feeding of the dog, and then he was back to work. He'd wasted enough time already.

Bob didn't intend to waste any more.

*

He hadn't worked so enthusiastically on a project in ages. Between lunch and tea Bob produced in the region of twenty prints based on the five "faulty" negatives. Close-ups, large scale blow-ups, details ... By 5 o'clock he'd done all he could with that batch. It was now a case of going out and seeing if he could get lucky again. Same spot, same time of day. In theory it should work.

Bob loaded up his bag with film, checked his Praktica over twice again just to make sure (he didn't dare swap it), and even slipped an automatic into his coat pocket.

Chappie jumped up and down as he headed towards the door.

"Not this time, fella. It's too important. I'll take you for a walk tomorrow. I promise." The dog cocked his head and whined, clearly wanting to go with Bob.

Or wanting him to stay.

And then he was off, making his way up the path to find those special hills. Before it was too late.

To his chagrin it took him longer than he thought it would to reach the place. Something was diverting him, holding him back. But he was determined, fuelled by a driving curiosity. He had to know. *Had to!*

By the time he arrived the sun was already quite low in the sky. Again he marvelled at the stunning cloud formations, the red streaks slicing them in halves, thirds and quarters. Nature's plan was wonderful to behold.

Bob raised his single lens reflex, took a light reading, adjusted the aperture, and clicked off a couple of shots. He couldn't see anything unusual, but then he hadn't seen anything the other night either. Best to make sure.

The sun was almost in position, the same height as it was on the photos (and he should know; he'd studied them hard enough). Bob lined up another shot and depressed the button. The shutter snapped across. Wind on, then again, wind on. As the shutter came back this time, Bob spotted a faint light through the glass. Now at last he had something to go on. If he could just get closer.

A kind of madness gripped him. Bob ran up the incline, camera still welded to his face. He could hear his own breathing in his head, fast and deep. A little bit further, a bit further—

Something caught his foot and sent him flying. He landed hard on the tough grass, rolling over to protect the camera. The bag dropped from his shoulder. There was a yelp.

Two eyes flashed, a panting noise: Chappie. Somehow he'd escaped from the cottage and followed on. Bob raised himself up.

"What are you doing here? Bad dog!" The canine growled, auburn fur erect on his back. Bob had never seen him like this before. Chappie was usually such a well-behaved pet.

He traced the dog's gaze, looking for something that could explain this abnormal behaviour. He soon found it.

There, walking across the hill, were the figures from his photos. Only now he saw them with the utmost clarity. Men, women, children, as white as milk. All trekking purposefully along. Bob still didn't know where they were going. Or what compelled them to proceed.

He was up and running again. In a replay of his dream, Bob reached out to the nearest one.

"Who are you? Where are you going?" he shouted, grabbing at its wrist.

The figure turned.

Didn't anyone tell you?

Chappie was barking from somewhere behind him. A far off sound.

You didn't ought …

There was no pulse in that wrist. Only coldness; an icy cold.

… to be hanging around …

No blood was being pumped through this being.

… up there …

Bob was looking into the eyes of a dead man.

… so near to nightfall …

A dead man with his face.

And now Bob became that man. He was part of The Procession, crammed between a pasty teenager with tattoos and a distraught woman holding a baby close to her chest, the tears streaming down her face. His fear became amazement as he gaped back along that line. It stretched out as far as he could see. There were thousands, no, millions of walkers, going on ad infinitum. And in front of him it was the same story. Bob could only guess, but it seemed to him that the cavalcade encircled the entire globe, invisible to all but a select few at select times, in select locations. The spirits of people who'd died during that day.

"I-I don't belong here. I have to go … " Yet even as he spoke the words, he knew how wrong he was.

Because at that precise moment he saw Chappie standing barking over his own limp body on the hill. Bob Greenan's neck was twisted, his black tongue protruding from his mouth. His precious camera still in his hands.

He acknowledged the call the others followed. A summons. Something dragging him along the peak. Blinkered like a shire horse, he strode on—his resplendent soul glowing brightly.

Bob's head was emptying. *Purged.* He'd wanted to know where they were going and soon he would find out …

As the sun disappeared behind that hill, a shroud of darkness covered the land. And when, in the morning, the shroud was lifted, there was nothing left of those spirits who had marched along in The Procession.

*

Ian Swain pulled up outside the cottage at 10am only to find Bob's dog Chappie scratching at the door. For a full five minutes Ian knocked and shouted for Bob, but no one answered. He assumed the photographer must have taken Chappie for a walk and the playful dog had got away from him somehow. Thankfully one of the windows round the back was open and Ian managed to scramble inside, cursing the fact he'd scuffed the knees of his expensive trousers.

The cottage was indeed empty; the bedroom, living room, the kitchen ... not a sign of life anywhere. Tired of waiting, Ian entered the darkroom. He began looking round for the pictures Bob had been raving about. Were they really as good as he made out?

But despite searching high and low, all he could find were a stack of prints on the desk, plus a few stills clipped to the drying line.

Ian inspected each piece in turn, pulling a face. Surely there had to be some kind of mistake. These were landscapes all right, Bob's speciality. But most were overexposed almost to the point of being black. And a couple, yes one or two at best, had big white splotches running across the middle where the camera had let in light at the back ...

Words to the Wise

In the beginning was the Word, and that was terrifying enough.

Then more words, sentences … the bastards gathering together, multiplying like vermin, swarming like insects. And just as hard to get rid of. You couldn't call in an exterminator to eliminate them, especially not then—not back in the day.

How did humans go from grunting at each other, from painting pictures on the cave walls, to communicating through language? Then writing this down on those same walls, the forefathers of kids who sprayed graffiti all over the brickwork of certain parts of the city where he grew up, little realising the real damage they were doing—the plague they were spreading.

Not that they were anywhere near as dangerous as the ones encased in board or leather. That came later, after the words and sentences. The pages, then the covers. Committing them to the ages, helping them to endure. Some people created prisons for the words, locking them with clasps which ran from front to back, holding the monstrosities inside. But eventually even they would be unfastened and read.

It made Samuel Kellerman shudder to even think about it. The very act of opening one of those things, letting out what was inside, speaking the—

When had it started for him? When had he begun to notice the power they had—not just to influence people, to influence *the world*, but also to destroy, to wreak their havoc?

As with most things, in those all-important formative years.

His first ever memories were of his parents sitting by the side of his bed, with one of those fucking torture devices resting on their laps. They'd open it, then begin translating what was there into sound. Releasing it into the air, its vileness so strong he'd almost been able to taste it.

The stories ... The tales they'd told, about far-off places, about monsters and heroes. Ostensibly, good would triumph over evil—but Samuel knew. Oh, how he knew. That once they'd been let out, those words, those stories couldn't be contained again. They'd remain in his room, invisible, only coming to life once his parents had gone again, turning out the lights—apart from that one nightlight which made everything seem so much worse.

The monsters they'd read about, all the ogres and dragons and witches and goblins, were suddenly there in the room with him, but no heroes were to be found. In real life heroes didn't exist; Samuel realised that at an early age, too. The words formed themselves into those creatures, somehow taking shape, using the dreaded language to mould themselves into something that could never be stopped. Something that wanted him so badly ...

He'd scream and scream, night after night—beg to be let into his parents' room. To sleep there so he would be safe; because the word-monsters very rarely attacked if you were in groups (though he suspected this did happen on occasion).

They'd sigh, but allow him in just to get some peace—then try to get him to settle the next night by opening more books, reading more stories. They just didn't get it, in spite of his trying to explain to them in his own way.

"What a vivid imagination," his mother would insist.

"*Too* vivid," his father would snap, bleary-eyed.

Samuel suspected he was the cause of his parents' break up, that they couldn't cope with his "strange ways". It was also probably the reason they'd distanced themselves from him as he grew up. Not that he could talk; he hadn't made much of an effort since his childhood to keep in touch either. He certainly didn't write them. Oh no.

It was the same thing at school, when they could actually force him to attend. School was full of the damned things, on shelves, inside desks, in backpacks. And that was before you even got to the library. He'd had to be physically restrained more than once when in class and the teachers would say, without thinking about it, "Would you all take out your books and turn to—"

That was it, he just had to get out.

Samuel was taken to see people, of course—men dressed in tweed, who talked at him as much as they did to him. Tried to get him to disclose his knowledge, tell them his secrets. Open up about his little "problem". They even gave it a name (which was hardly accurate): bibliophobia. But after many sessions, when they were considering sending him away for treatment—and especially after they'd caught him with those matches (he'd just wanted to burn a few of the things, an ultimately futile, but token, gesture ... they would have gone up so easily)—he figured out it was best to try and hide his fears, pretend everything was all right. Even though this was so very far from the truth. They'd still catch him, however, those men in tweed—glancing sideways at the books on their shelves. Wriggling in the chair under their harsh gaze. That army of hardbacks.

Because the non-fiction was as dangerous as the fiction, Samuel had figured out. Probably more so, because it could influence you on an even greater level under the guise of legitimacy.

One of those men in tweed once said to him, "It's people who write down the words, who write the books. It's how we make sense of the world. They come from us."

And yes, in a sense they did. But the books, once opened, also fed us and infected us, perpetuating this vicious circle of contamination. Make sense of the world? It was how the ultimate chaos was caused! Samuel would have been happier living in a society where everyone was struck dumb and had their hands cut off at birth. At least then there would be no way of it getting out ... the sickness. Most of the words would remain between those covers—or would they?

In his dreams, Samuel could hear the rustle of the leaves, imagined that they could worm their way out on their own; prise open their coffins like vampires and climb out; slithering in chains of letters like snakes, to wrap themselves around you. His worst nightmares would revolve around being pulled into their world, the one created by them, facilitated by human beings. A black magic kingdom, a hell in which they languished and were the masters of.

It was a wonder he hadn't gone stark, staring mad by his late teens. But he'd been stronger than that, got a handle on it and learnt to cope with those monstrosities that seemed to be all around him, wherever he turned. He'd minimise the risk as much as he could, but how could you escape it, really? They were everywhere, like oxygen. He couldn't even go into a supermarket without being confronted with them down at least one of the aisles, or even at the check-out: paperbacks "on special offer!" They were "special" all right.

He wanted to scream at the people around him: "Why can't you fucking well see it? The danger you're in ... No, don't pick that up, don't open—" His hand would be on the matches in his pocket—his only protection—by this point.

But what was the use? It seemed he was the only one who knew their true nature, everyone else had been brainwashed.

Yes, he was the only one wise to their game.

He decided once his eighteenth birthday had passed that an urban environment probably wasn't the best bet for him, so he moved to one of the quietest places he could find. Out into the countryside, where there was an abundance of the raw material used to make those blasted things, but still in its natural form; the rustling of a different kind of leaves in the light breeze here.

Samuel found work on a local farm, which helped him pay the rent at a local boarding house. Everyone was friendly enough, and though he couldn't guarantee not encountering one of his enemies, at least he wasn't seeing them on the subway, or posters of them plastered everywhere. It was an occasional encounter, not day-to-day. And the most he'd have to deal with at the nearby shop were the magazines and newspapers, which were on the far side, away from the food and drink anyway.

He spent his days working hard out in the fields, enjoying everything nature had to offer. There was nothing quite like toiling against a backdrop of rolling green hills, under a blue sky and full, yellow sun, to re-energise you.

His nights were more peaceful. Samuel had requested when he first moved in that the TV set be taken out of his room at the boarding house.

"Prefer to read, eh?" said his landlady, Mrs Mathis, who had a face like a scrunched up tissue.

The smile Samuel gave her in reply was more like a grimace. He couldn't watch TV, because the channels played shows and films *based* on books. It was second-hand, filtered through directors and producers, but at the heart of that so-called entertainment were the words. From books, to screenplays, to the eye.

He'd never owned a computer or mobile phone. Emails and texts were as alien to Samuel as breathing underwater. Just as hazardous, as far as he was concerned.

He went on like this for some time, confident he was avoiding their attentions. He'd even started going to the local public house, *The Lion & Lamb*, every now and again for a drink. They had no TV in the corner, unlike some pubs, and preferred to hang paintings and photos on the walls rather than line them with ticking time-bombs in the form of reading matter.

Samuel hung out with the residents of the village, played games of dominoes, darts and pool, and generally enjoyed his life. He was known as the "quiet one" because he very rarely engaged in trivial conversation, didn't waste his (didn't like to use) words. But generally he was happy ... for a while. Something was missing, though; something had *always* been missing.

He found out what that was when he caught sight of her one day.

There had been other girls ... women ... in the village, in *The Lion & Lamb*, but Samuel had never really been interested. For one thing in a place like this—where the ratio of male to female was something like fifty to one—most of them were already taken. But not her; not yet, anyway.

Samuel first saw her strolling through the village one Saturday afternoon. He'd been on his way to the shop to pick up supplies for the weekend, and stopped dead in his tracks. Her long, brown hair was only just held back with a headband—curls escaping from the side as she bounded happily down the street. Her face was like something out of a renaissance painting, skin pale but fresh, cheeks alive with colour. She was wearing a white summer dress with red spots, kitten heels on her feet. Samuel felt his heart stop, then start again, then beat faster than before.

She had to be new to the village, because he'd never seen her here—and he'd seen all of the villagers many, many times over the years. She caught him staring at her and glanced away, then back again. He hadn't moved, but his mouth was gaping open. Heaven knows what he must have looked like, but when he saw her frowning he closed his mouth and attempted a smile; a much better one than he'd given Mrs Mathis when he first moved here.

To his surprise, she smiled back; then began making her way over.

Samuel felt his heart beating faster than ever, faster even than when he'd been alone in his room as a child and those word-monsters had—

"Hello," she called, as she finished crossing the street—holding up her hand to shade her eyes (which he now noticed were hazel-coloured). "Do I know you from somewhere?"

Samuel couldn't speak. Wasn't used to it anyway. He simply nodded, then shook his head.

She laughed. "Which is it?"

He knew what she meant, that it felt like they'd met before but hadn't. It was weird, and he didn't know how to explain it. So, finding his voice from somewhere, he blurted: "No, but ... "

"You really do seem familiar to me. Did you go to school around here?"

Another shake of the head, firmer this time. So she'd gone to school in the village ... Maybe moved away and returned? He savoured every new little piece of information about her.

"That's really strange. I'm Leah. Leah Russell," she told him, as if it might jolt his memory.

"S-Samuel," he managed.

She smiled again, wider this time. "I like that. Samuel ... Sammy."

He shook his head again. "Samuel," he repeated, more emphatically. Sammy reminded him of his youth and he didn't want that, not now ... not ever.

"Okay, Samuel it is, then." But she would never remember, and always called him Sammy. "Look, I've just moved back in around here and this is all a bit of a culture shock for me. A lot of things are the same, but there's so much that's changed. Would you mind maybe showing me around a bit?"

Heart still beating out of his chest, Samuel had agreed. They spent the rest of that afternoon touring the village, with Leah doing most of the talking, to be honest. She didn't seem to mind Samuel being quiet, and he didn't mind hearing more about her as they walked: the fact that she'd lived here for a few years of her childhood, fostered out to a couple who were now long-since dead; the fact she had always wanted to come back because she enjoyed the peace and quiet, although still rented out a place in a town not far away because she worked there—in a small museum, containing objects from the place's past which she found fascinating. Samuel took all this in, growing increasingly fascinated with her. "I'm on a bit of an extended leave at the moment, while I get sorted out here."

They ended up in *The Lion & Lamb* that evening and he couldn't help but notice the looks Leah drew from the other men. But they found a secluded corner, and talked some more ... well, Leah did ... until it was closing time, and then he walked her back to her place: a cottage on the outskirts of the village.

"Well, thanks for a lovely day, Sammy ... Samuel," she said. "I hope we can do it again sometime. I would invite you in, but I'm still getting straight inside."

He nodded once more, and she kissed him on the cheek. Samuel didn't remember the walk back to his own home.

The next couple of weeks passed in much the same way, with them seeing each other as often as possible—fitting it around his work at the farm. Samuel caught her eying him up a few times as he stacked bales of hay with his shirt off. "You really are a bit of a discovery, Sammy," she told him as she picked him up in her little Ford Ka.

She wanted to know how come he'd chosen that profession; he was a bright young man, after all. And it was true, the farmer had asked if he wanted to help with the more administrative side of things—like keeping the books. Keep them? Samuel would rather have cooked them. Burned them!

He told Leah he just preferred the simpler way of life.

Then the night came when she did invite him in to her cottage. "It's still a bit of a mess, I just haven't got around to unloading most of it," Leah explained, flicking back a rogue strand of curly hair. She hadn't been wrong, most of her belongings were still in crates and boxes, giving the place a ... simpler look about it. Samuel pulled a face when he saw the laptop open on her coffee table, however, but she moved it out of the way so they could sit down and enjoy the wine she'd fetched. "Maybe you could ... help me get things straight here," she suggested. "Move some of the furniture and stuff. I mean, it's not as if you're a weakling, is it?" And with that, she moved closer to him on the couch, hand running over the muscles of his arm, feeling his chest through the thin cotton shirt he had on.

Feeling his racing heart.

Before he knew what was happening, Samuel was in bed with Leah. He didn't have any time to worry about her being his first, and if she noticed then she certainly didn't say anything. "That was amazing," Leah said afterwards, laying back panting. "I don't know ... it just feels right with you, Sammy. I've never had that before."

Samuel smiled, and the nightmares left him alone that night.

It wouldn't be long before they returned again, a week or so later when Samuel called round to help with Leah's unpacking. She asked him to carry one of the heavy boxes upstairs, but he tripped on a piece of loose carpet, dropping the cardboard container on its edge—where it split. They pushed their way out, hardbacks and paperbacks alike, and Samuel recoiled, biting back the scream in his throat—hand indistinctively going to his pocket where he kept his matches.

Stupid ... stupid, stupid, *stupid!* He'd been an idiot to think she wouldn't have books packed, someone like Leah. Just because he hadn't seen any so far. She had no TV, or just hadn't got around to getting one for this place. It made sense that she'd need to do something to pass the time, when she wasn't with him.

"Sammy? Sammy, what is it?" asked Leah, meeting him as he rushed to the base of the stairs.

"*Samuel!*" he barked at her. "My name is Samuel!" Then he collapsed into her arms and began sobbing.

After he'd made her take the box of books outside, while he sat curled up in the corner of the living room, hand still on his pocket, he explained what was wrong. It was probably the longest he'd ever spoken to Leah; everything just came tumbling out. When he'd finished, breathing hard, he looked at her for a response. For that smile he'd seen the first day he'd met her. It was conspicuous by its absence—her expression a mixture of shock and disgust.

"But ... but surely there are people you could see about this," she began.

He shook his head. He'd been there, done that, bought the fucking T-shirt, mug and badge. "I-I should go," he said, rising, but she'd placed her hand on his arm.

"We'll figure this out," she told him. "I promise you. Sam ... Samuel, I love you." Then she smiled and he felt like everything really was going to be all right.

"I love you too," he told her, then they held each other.

Leah's sabbatical ended not long after that, and though they kept on seeing each other when she was back at the cottage— now devoid of her collection of books ("They're evil, Leah. You have to get rid of them ... ")—she was gone for longer and longer periods. Work, she said. At the museum.

Samuel missed Leah so, so much—it wasn't as if he could phone her up, or email or text. On more than a few visits, she mentioned a guy called Trevor, who worked at the museum and was the cleverest person she knew. "He thinks there are things you could do."

"You've talked about me to someone?"

"I had to," she said, tears welling in her eyes. "All this is a lot to handle on my own." Samuel's face wrinkled up worse than Mrs Mathis', but she continued. "There are therapies, things you could do to have a normal life. So we could have a normal life."

He felt like saying, "What? Destroy all the fucking books in the world? Get rid of every sentence, word, everything with writing on, anywhere? Stop people writing it all down?" Instead he offered: "But we could ... we do have a life, don't we? Like this?"

When her eyes dipped, he knew she wanted more. For him, for them both.

Samuel began to suspect something might be going on with this Trevor, the way she talked about him all the time when she was back, the way the bloke reckoned he could cure Samuel—like he knew what he was fucking talking about. It was more to impress Leah than anything, he suspected.

"I want you to come and meet him," Leah said one weekend. "Just hear what he has to say."

Samuel grunted, but reluctantly agreed. He did want to meet this man, if only to check out what all the fuss was about. Eye up the competition. Of course, it would mean going into the town, but he'd have Leah at least to lean on. "Straight to the museum in the car," she promised. "Then straight back again."

He'd made it from the car park to the museum with little difficulty, in spite of a bus going by advertising the latest bestseller. Inside, Samuel could see why Leah liked it here: the objects from the past in glass cabinets (don't think about the panels of writing beneath them), the old photographs just like they had back at *The Lion & Lamb*. People doing an honest day's work, in mines, at factories, on farms.

"Just down here," Leah said, waving her hand to a set of steps.

Samuel descended cautiously, then walked into the corridor below. The light was dimmer down here, shadowy. Trevor's office was the room at the end, she told him, following.

He opened the door and stepped inside.

Samuel was halfway in before he even realised where he was. Then he was pushed further inside, by stronger hands than Leah's. The door slammed behind him, locks turning.

"No ... " he breathed, then turned and banged on the door. "No, please ... let me out!"

"It's for your own good," came a voice through the door. A man's voice. Trevor ... who still had no face to Samuel.

Samuel turned back round again, saw the rows and rows of books in this basement, the half-light throwing shadows across the room.

"We have one of the biggest collections of fiction and non-fiction in the district, all donated by the public," said the voice. "You might as well make yourself comfortable, you're going to be in there a while."

"Leah?" Her name was a wail.

"I'm sorry, Samuel," came her voice eventually, "but Trevor says you need to confront your fear to overcome it."

"*No!*" shouted Samuel, banging on the door again, "you don't understand what you're doing! What you've done!" Already he could hear the rustle of the pages, so many pages of so many books. He was the lamb, and they were about to leave him in the lion's den.

"It's the only way," sobbed Leah. "The only way to cure you."

Cure me? thought Samuel. *You're going to kill me!*

Kill or cure, kill or cure ...

He could hear footsteps receding, Trevor probably dragging Leah away so she wouldn't have to listen to Samuel's pleas. This wasn't like going cold turkey, he wasn't an addict. His fear was completely real and now he knew that she had become infected too, all those years of reading. He'd been kidding himself to think she was okay. That he could trust her.

Samuel turned, hand going to the pocket where his matches were. Fumbling, he felt inside and brought out the box.

Then something touched his leg and he began to scream even louder than when he was a child.

*

Leah lay on the bed, unable to sleep.

In the months that had passed since they'd tried to help Samuel everything had changed. She heard the heavy breathing of the figure, the lump of a man beside her. Trevor ... who she'd turned to only after Samuel—

No, it had been her fault. She'd listened to Trevor in the first place, his cod psychology, that you had to face what you were scared of to be free of it. Well, now she was free of Samuel, and not a day had gone by that she didn't miss him.

When they'd returned to the basement library, after several hours—and night had fallen—everything was silent. To begin with Leah thought Samuel might have passed out. "What if he's really hurt inside there?" she'd said, biting her lip. What if he'd done something to *himself?* she meant. Maybe his phobia ran much deeper than either of them imagined—it had sounded silly to her, especially with her love of books, her aspirations to maybe one day become a writer (banging away on that laptop of hers, getting so far in and then giving up).

When they'd opened the door, they found books everywhere— on the floor, open and hanging from the shelves. Some looked like they'd had pages ripped out of them, others were dented as if they'd been punched.

Leah stepped forward and something crunched beneath her feet. She bent down and picked up a match. She saw more of them now, scattered about down there, the box some distance away, as if it had been knocked from a hand.

Christ, what had she done? If Samuel had lit one of those ...

But he hadn't. And there was no sign of him, either. They looked everywhere in that room, called his name. Nothing.

"He must have got out through the vent," said Trevor, pointing up to the shaft on the far wall. It looked knackered at the best of times, so might have been removed (though why replace it again?). But surely it was too small for anyone to squeeze through?

In a panic, desperate to get away? Samuel might have—

In her gut, Leah didn't really believe that, but it made the most logical sense. In any event, she hadn't seen Samuel since. They drove round the city, looking on the streets, but saw nothing. He wasn't back at the village—Mrs Mathis hadn't seen or heard from him when Leah returned. Neither had they seen him up at the farm.

By the following week, his job was gone and his room let out to someone else.

Leah hadn't been able to stay in that village, too many memories from the previous summer. So she'd moved back to the flat in town, putting the cottage up for sale again before she'd even got to know it that well. Unlike Samuel. She'd known—or thought she'd known—him so well. It wasn't till later that she understood why. He was like so many characters she'd read about, an amalgamation of the heroes from her favourite books: the strong, silent type. And he was such a good listener ...

(Had something somehow engineered their meeting?)

He was also the character she wrote about as her male lead, more often than not. The perfect man—and now he was gone forever, leaving her with Trevor. He began to snore as she lay there, listening. Unable to sleep because of the nightmares.

Nightmares like the ones Samuel had told her about, where she saw his death over and over again in that basement library.

Saw him fighting off the books as they flew from the shelves, saw chains of words snaking from inside them, tugging at his leg, yanking the matches from his grasp, pulling him apart and then absorbing him into their pages.

In the past, she would have read if she couldn't sleep—but the battered paperback she'd begun a couple of months ago was shut away in her bedside table after she'd fancied she'd seen the words emerging from the page as she read one night (after too much Merlot, admittedly). Imagined she'd seen them form into shapes, figures ... maybe even monsters.

She'd slammed the book closed, then heard the rustling of the others on the shelves. The books she told Samuel she'd got rid of, but had really only been hiding from him. How could she part with her beloved collection?

She was thinking about doing just that, though, lately. Having them around was making her just too uneasy.

You should write about all this, she told herself. *Turn it into a story; might even finish it this time, might even get somewhere with it.*

But wasn't that what they wanted, the living words that had killed Samuel, or kept him locked up inside their worlds even now because he knew the truth? If she fictionalised all that, wouldn't she be drawing attention away from the danger? Making fictions from fact, just as they made fact from fictions. She was starting to wise up now, wasn't she. Starting to see how right Sammy had been, how horrific the act she'd allowed to happen—

Leah heard the rustling again, drew the bedclothes up to her chin like she was a little girl once more, afraid of the shadows.

Trevor continued to snore, but the rustling was drowning him out.

"In the beginning," she whispered, "was the word."

And it would be there at the end as well, even after they were all gone—when it had done what it needed to do with people.

In the beginning, was the Word, a whispering voice repeated.

And that was terrifying enough …

About the Author

Paul Kane is an award-winning, bestselling writer and editor based in Derbyshire, UK. His short story collections include *Alone (In the Dark)*, *Touching the Flame*, *FunnyBones*, *Peripheral Visions*, *Shadow Writer*, *The Adventures of Dalton Quayle*, *The Butterfly Man and Other Stories*, *The Spaces Between*, *Ghosts*, the British Fantasy Award-nominated *Monsters*, *Shadow Casting*, *Nailbiters*, *Death*, *Disexistence*, *Scary Tales*, *More Monsters*, *Lost Souls* and *The Controllers*. His novellas include *The Lazarus Condition*, *RED* and *Pain Cages* (a #1 Amazon bestseller). He is the author of such novels as *Of Darkness and Light*, *The Gemini Factor* and the bestselling *Arrowhead* trilogy (*Arrowhead*, *Broken Arrow* and *Arrowland*, gathered together in the sell-out omnibus edition *Hooded Man*), a post-apocalyptic reworking of the Robin Hood mythology. His latest novels include *Lunar* (which is set to be turned into a feature film), the short Y.A. novel *The Rainbow Man* (as P.B. Kane), the critically-acclaimed and award-winning *Sherlock Holmes and the Servants of Hell* from Solaris, the sequels to *RED*—*Blood RED* and *Deep RED*—*Before* from Grey Matter Press (a Top 5 Amazon bestseller in Dark Fantasy), *Arcana* from WordFire Press and *Her Last Secret* from HQ Digital/ HarperCollins (as P.L. Kane).

He has also written for comics, most notably for the *Dead Roots* zombie anthology alongside writers such as James Moran (*Torchwood*, *Cockneys vs. Zombies*) and Jason Arnopp (*Doctor Who*, *Friday the 13th*, *The Last Days of Jack Sparks*) and as part of the team turning *Clive Barker's Books of Blood* into motion comics for Seraphim/MadeFire. His stand-alone comic *The Disease*, published by Hellbound Media, was also a 2016 Ghastly Award-nominated title in the "One Shot" category. Paul is co-editor of the anthology *Hellbound Hearts* (Simon & Schuster)—stories based around the mythology that spawned *Hellraiser*—*The Mammoth Book of Body Horror* (Constable & Robinson/Running Press), featuring the likes of Stephen King and James Herbert, *A Carnivàle of Horror* (PS) featuring Ray Bradbury and Joe Hill, *Beyond Rue Morgue* from Titan, stories based around Poe's detective, Dupin, and *Exit Wounds*—also from Titan—a crime anthology featuring the likes of Lee Child, Val McDermid, Dennis Lehane and Jeffery Deaver.

His non-fiction books include *The Hellraiser Films and Their Legacy*, *Voices in the Dark* and *Shadow Writer—The Non-Fiction. Vol. 1: Reviews* and *Vol. 2: Articles and Essays*, plus his genre journalism has appeared in the likes of *SFX*, *Fangoria*, *Dreamwatch*, *Gorezone*, *Rue Morgue* and *DeathRay*. He also co-wrote the afterword to the latest edition of Stephen King's *Night Shift* collection. He has been a Guest at Alt.Fiction five times, was a Guest at the first SFX Weekender, at Thought Bubble in 2011, Derbyshire Literary Festival and Off the Shelf in 2012, Monster Mash and Event Horizon in 2013, Edge-Lit in 2014 and 2018, HorrorCon, HorrorFest and Grimm Up North in 2015, The Dublin Ghost Story Festival and Sledge-Lit in 2016, IMATS Olympia and Celluloid Screams in 2017, plus Black Library Live and The UK Ghost Story Festival in 2019, as well as being a panellist at FantasyCon and the World Fantasy Convention, and a fiction judge at the Sci-Fi London Film Festival. He is a former Special Publications Editor of the British Fantasy Society and is currently serving as co-chair for the UK arm of the Horror Writers Association.

His work has been optioned for film and television, and his zombie story "Dead Time" was turned into an episode of the Lionsgate/NBC TV series *Fear Itself*, adapted by Steve Niles (*30 Days of Night*) and directed by Darren Lynn Bousman (*SAW II-IV*). He also scripted *The Opportunity*, which premiered at the Cannes Film Festival, *Wind Chimes* (directed by Brad *"Hallows Eve"* Watson and which sold to TV), *The Weeping Woman*—filmed by award-winning director Mark Steensland, starring Tony-nominated actor Stephen Geoffreys (*Fright Night*)—*Confidence*, directed by award-winning Mike Clarke (*A Hand to Play, Paper and Plastic*) which stars Simon Bamford (*Hellraiser, Nightbreed, Starfish*), and *The Torturer* directed by Joe Manco of Little Spark Films. His work for audio includes the full cast drama adaptation of *The Hellbound Heart* for Bafflegab, starring Tom Meeten (*The Ghoul*), Neve McIntosh (*Doctor Who*) and Alice Lowe (*Prevenge*), and the *Robin of Sherwood* adventure *The Red Lord* for Spiteful Puppet/ITV, narrated by Ian Ogilvy (*Return of the Saint*). You can find out more at his website www.shadow-writer.co.uk which has featured Guest Writers such as Dean Koontz, Robert Kirkman, Charlaine Harris and Guillermo del Toro.

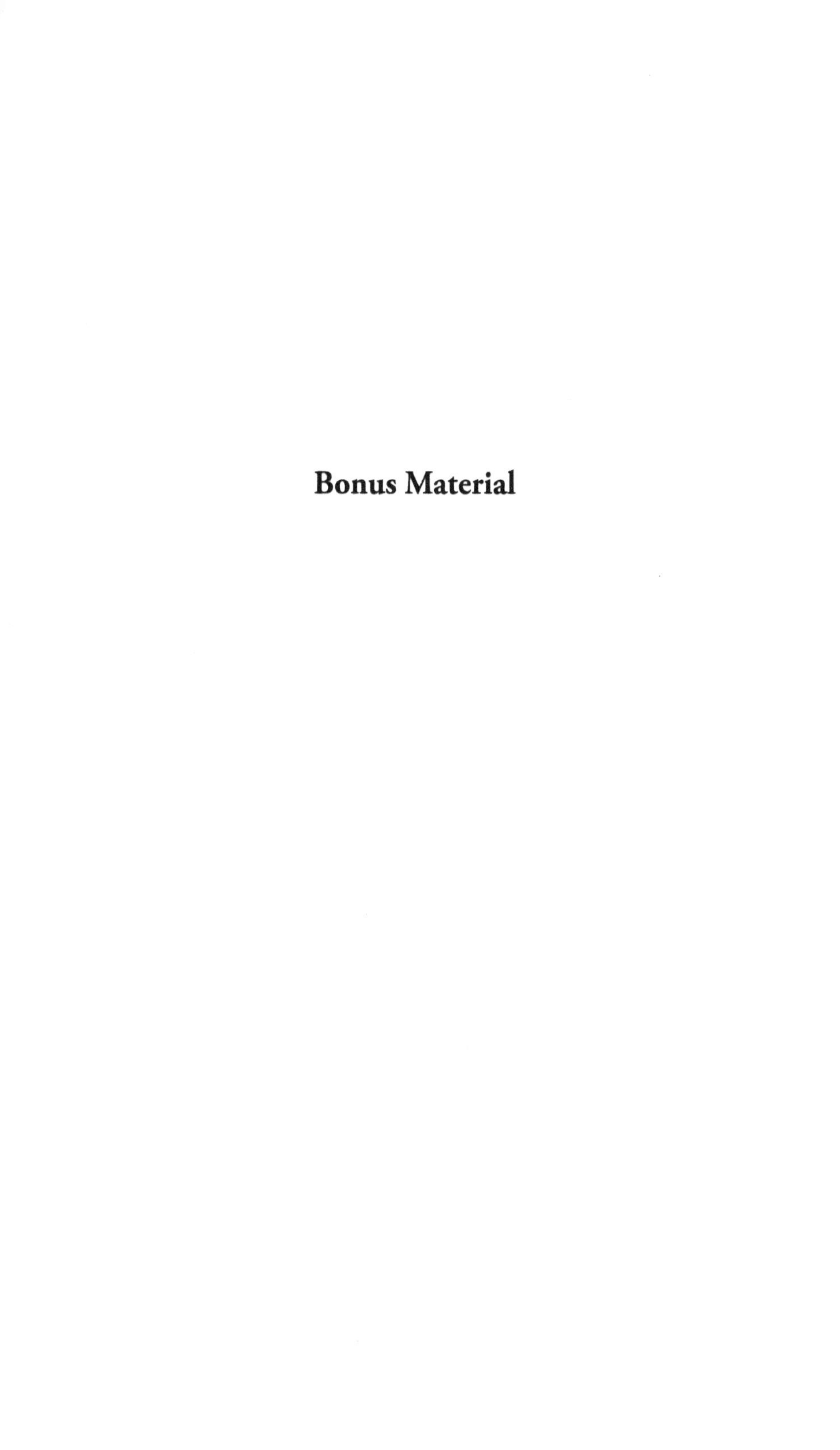

Bonus Material

From Page To Screen… And Back Again
By Paul Kane

I've been a film fan all my life – my BA and MA are both in Film Studies, and I've been known to script the odd short movie or two … very odd sometimes! So imagine my delight when in January 2018 I was contacted by Loose Canon films to see if I'd written any stories in the folk horror sub-genre. And *of course* my answer was yes, I've done a fair few; I absolutely love folk horror! *The Wicker Man* is definitely in my top ten all-time horror movies, and in recent years films like *The Ritual* (based on a novel by my old mate Adam Nevill) and *Midsommer* have counted amongst my favourites. I'm even, as I write this, taking my cue from folk horror for the third of my thrillers for HQ/Harper as PL Kane.

But anyway, back to the story … I sent a number of shorts over, including "Men of the Cloth" a tale revolving around an isolated English village and creepy scarecrows (which you'll probably now have read in this very book), inspired by my time teaching out in the community for a further education college.

Imagine how my delight turned into excitement when Andy Collier and Tor Mian of LC wanted to meet up the following month and discuss adapting that particular novelette into a feature. My better half Marie (O'Regan, an extremely talented writer and editor herself) and I spent a terrific day – where else, but in a pub; *all* the best meetings take place there! – chatting with Andy and Tor. We talked, not only about the possible film but all things genre-related, and had terrific time. They asked me at that one if I minded them altering the tale for their script, which I didn't at all. I've had some experience of my work changing when it's adapted into other mediums, especially from page to screen: most memorably when the zombie romp "Dead Time" became

New Year's Day for NBC/Lions Gate's *Fear Itself*. And, to me, it usually results in something very interesting indeed. I really love seeing how other people approach your stuff. Writing's quite a solitary business, so I for one always enjoy collaborating or seeing what other creatives can do with the seeds of your narrative and characters: in this instance, transplanting the action to Norway, paring the family down to a couple – the wife being pregnant – and making it Lovecraftian, something I definitely had no problem with. Oh, and giving it a new title, which I fell in love with instantly: *The Colour of Madness*.

Then imagine how my excitement shot through the roof when I was told genre legend Barbara Crampton – no stranger to Lovecraftian horrors herself, having starred in Stuart Gordon's *Re-Animator* and *From Beyond* – had been brought on board! I'll just let that settle in for a moment. Barbara. Crampton. In something based on my work! I've been a fan of Barbara's work for so long, and this was simply a dream come true. At the time of penning this piece the feature is in the can, as they say – you might have seen me sharing lots of behind the scenes photos from the production company Hyrda Films on my social media (though you're about to see some more exclusive ones here). The bulk of the shoot took place over the summer of 2019, and it is currently in post-production.

I caught up with Andy again at a HWA pub meet in September 2019, after a signing Marie and I did for our Titan anthology *Wonderland* at Forbidden Planet, Shaftsbury Avenue. He'd just got back to this country, and we got chatting again over yet more beers; by a strange coincidence the London bar we were in served a very nice Norwegian ale, which Andy introduced me to. And so the idea of doing some kind of tie-in cropped up, which would include not only the original story and some of the other ones I pitched – plus my own aquatic Lovecraftian piece "Thicker Than Water" – but also certain extras, including extracts from the script and more of those behind the scenes photos I mentioned before.

I told Andy I'd just had a book published by the superb Luna Press, who had been a joy to work with, and that *The Controllers* had a similar formant: a collection with extras, including a gallery and hand-written scans. We both got excited at that point and when I returned home again I pitched to Francesca and Rob, who were equally as excited about the notion… The upshot was the project that you're holding in your hot little hands, timed to coincide with the movie coming out – and with a cover based on an original poster. The whole thing going from page to screen, and back again!

It's my dearest hope that you guys are as excited about the release – of both the feature and this official movie tie-in – as we all are. A hell of way to start not just a new year in 2020, but a whole new decade!

Until next time, as the tagline to *The Colour of Madness* says: Dream well.

Paul Kane
Derbyshire, December 2019.

Shared DNA
By Andy Collier

The movie of *The Colour of Madness* was very much inspired by Paul's short story and the shared DNA is very strong, but cosmetically there are some obvious differences between the two.

First the crazy, cranked-up-to-eleven ending of "Men of the Cloth" would have been difficult to film convincingly (especially on a budget!) so we needed to amend that.

Secondly, the old adage "never work with children or animals" drew us to replace the kids in the story with a latex baby bump. But the sense of threat to the unborn child remains.

Other changes… we made the story more explicitly Lovecraftian by replacing Paul's Green Man style-creature with an unnamed entity that bears a striking resemblance to Cthulhu. And once we went fully Lovecraftian, setting the story in a remote Norwegian settlement between the mountains and the sea just seemed to work. The amazing scenery provides free production value.

Norse mythology and the Cthulhu mythos have some nice little parallels (are the halls of the dead in Valhalla, or R'lyeh?!). And what happened to the Norse settlement in Greenland that vanished without trace a thousand years ago? Most theories blame it upon a mini ice age, but can some interference by the Inuit cultists mentioned in "The Call of Cthulhu" really be ruled out so easily?!

Overall, the movie was super fun to make and I'd like to thank Paul for giving us such an unsettling piece of source material.

Keep 'em coming...

Andy Collier
(co-writer and co-director of The Colour of Madness)
London, January 2020

Script Extracts by Andy Collier & Tor Mian

19   INT. PUB. NIGHT   19

ECU of hundreds of tiny bubbles rising through
amber liquid. SOUND is abstract aquatic noise.

Rack focus to pub customers sitting around the
beer glass we are looking through.

Brief pan and then we rack focus to the door.
ISAAC and EMMA enter.

The pub is dotted with locals. Fishermen in
jumpers and jeans.

They pay no attention to ISAAC and EMMA as they
take in their surroundings.

EMMA rubs her back, in obvious discomfort due to
her condition.

LEDVOR, the middle-aged owner, locks eyes with
ISAAC as he rests his hands on the bar.

                    ISAAC
          Hello. Do you speak English?

LEDVOR replies in clear and precise English.

                    LEDVOR
          That depends.

ISAAC is baffled by this oxymoronic response.

                    ISAAC
          Depends? On what?

                    LEDVOR
          Do you speak Norwegian?

                    ISAAC
          Uh- no. I don't. I'm sorry-

                    LEDVOR
          (Slow. Deliberate. Patronising.)
          So if I don't speak English... and if you
          don't speak Norwegian... then how could we
          communicate?

LEDVOR shakes his head. Turns away to face a busy
table of regulars across the room. Shouts.

                    LEDVOR (CONT'D)
                  (Norwegian)
          Jaevla tourister! (Fucking tourists!)

There is a murmur of laughter from around the
bar. LEDVOR is obviously enjoying being able to
publicly "troll" his unwanted guests.

LEDVOR turns back to the bar and feigns an
expression of displeasure that ISAAC is still
standing there.

He lifts a heavy copper drip tray off the bar,
spits disgustedly on one corner of it and stabs
at it with a dirty cloth.

                    ISAAC
          So... you do speak English?!

                    LEDVOR
          Of course I speak English! Everybody
          speaks English! We raped your women...

LEDVOR chooses this particularly inappropriate
moment to eye EMMA up and down.

EMMA instinctively tightens her coat around
herself. LEDVOR looks back at ISAAC.

                    LEDVOR
          You raped our linguistic legacy.

                    ISAAC
          Er... actually I'm American. I don't think
          you guys made it that far.

                    LEDVOR
          What?

LEDVOR stares back at ISAAC with incredulity.
It's like somebody has just insulted his mother-
but he can't quite believe it.

                    LEDVOR (CONT'D)
          I take it you have never actually read a
          history book?

                    GUNNAR
                    (O.S)
          Is this man bothering you?

Both ISAAC and LEDVOR turn to look at GUNNAR- the
hulking man seated at the side of the bar.

                    LEDVOR
          His ignorance is bothering me that's for
          sure!

GUNNAR rises from his stool and strolls towards
ISAAC.

If it wasn't for his modern casual clothing you
would think he had stepped right out of a Norse
Saga.

Like all the Norwegians we meet, his English is
very fluent beneath a soft Norwegian accent. Eight
years of school, a steady trickle of tourists
brave enough to venture this far off the beaten

track and a lifetime of Hollywood movies.

                    GUNNAR
          So you're one of those indoctrinated
          Zombies that still thinks Christopher
          Columbus discovered America?

Everybody apart from ISAAC and EMMA laugh. EMMA
looks around uncomfortably.

ISAAC smiles nervously.

                    ISAAC
          Well... that depends on what you mean by
          'discovered'. Many would argue that the
          Native Americans actually discovered...

GUNNAR scoffs

                    GUNNAR
          We were smashing Cherokee Fitte when
          Christopher Columbus's great great many-
          times-great grandfather was suckling at
          his mother's teat.

ISAAC looks at his pregnant wife and then back at
the hulking man standing before him.

GUNNAR may tower over him and ISAAC may be trying
to maintain a friendly demeanor but he is not
easily intimidated.

                    ISAAC
          Gentleman... please. There's a lady
          present.

GUNNAR laughs as he looks EMMA up and down.

                    GUNNAR
          Oh I'm sorry. I didn't realize it was

                    glandular?

                         ISAAC
               Glandular?

                         GUNNAR
               I thought she was pregnant! Not just fat.
               Apologies. My mistake.

EMMA looks more and more uncomfortable with every
moment.

                         ISAAC
               She is pregnant...

                         GUNNAR
               Well, unless it was an immaculate
               conception I'm pretty sure at this stage
               she knows what a good harpooning is!

There are audible sniggers throughout the room.

ISAAC scans the various smirking faces around the
pub. His eyes rest back on GUNNAR.

                         ISAAC
                        (Sternly)
               That's not the point.

                         LEDVOR
                        (Norwegian)
               Det er ikke det hun sa! (That's not what
               she said!)

All the patrons laugh uproariously at this
childish and crude joke.

ISAAC'S unease is fading and being replaced with
anger.

                    EMMA
     Come on. Let's go. We can find somewhere
     else to eat.

                   LEDVOR
     Good luck with that...

EMMA tugs on ISAAC'S arm but he doesn't budge.
Now they really do have his back up.

He looks LEDVOR in the eye.

                   ISAAC
     We're not going anywhere. I'm hungry. He's
     going to feed us. Where's your menu?

LEDVOR returns his gaze.

                   LEDVOR
     We don't have a menu.

                   ISAAC
                (Frustrated)
     Of course you don't. But this is a fishing
     village right? I assume you serve fish?

                   LEDVOR
     We don't serve chili dogs and pizza if
     that's what you're looking for.

                   ISAAC
                (Trying to remain calm)
     No. Fish'll do fine. Do you have any
     Calamari?

The pub suddenly goes deathly silent.

ISAAC has clearly made some kind of faux pas. He
looks around confused.

                    LEDVOR
                   (Serious)
          Calamari is not a fish.

LEDVOR looks at ISAAC pointedly.

                    GUNNAR
                   (Deadpan)
          A fish is a vertebrate. Calamari is an
          invertebrate.

                    LEDVOR
                  (Pointedly)
          A fish has a backbone.

                    ISAAC
          It's seafood. Same thing.

                    GUNNAR
                 (Incredulous)
          Same thing?

                    ISAAC
          Yeah. It's seafood. You serve food from
          the sea. If you don't serve Calamari...

LEDVOR cuts him off.

                    LEDVOR
          We definitely don't serve Calamari.

ISAAC is losing his patience.

                    ISAAC
          Well, for the love of God what do you
          serve?

Beat.

                    LEDVOR
                   (Deadpan)
          That depends.

                    ISAAC
                  (Frustrated)
          Jesus Christ...

                    GUNNAR
          Jesus won't help you here...

EMMA tugs at ISAAC'S arm again.

                    EMMA
          Come on... Let's go...

                    GUNNAR
                  (Dismissive)
          Do what your lady tells you...

ISAAC clenches his jaw. He is trying to remain
calm but it is becoming a losing battle.

                    ISAAC
          We're not going anywhere. I'm hungry. You
          are going to feed us.

     GUNNAR looks ISAAC directly in the eye.

  ISAAC stares back at him with controlled menace.

                    GUNNAR
          I'll feed you to the sharks.

He takes a pull from his beer and then thumps
the empty bottle down onto the bar, screwing it
into the wooden surface as if it will never move
again.

EMMA holds onto ISAAC'S arm.

                    EMMA
          Isaac!

ISAAC holds GUNNAR'S stare, despite the Norwegian
having an eight-inch height advantage and arms
like knotted tree trunks.

ISAAC is clearly not the type of person to back
down from a fight... and with every passing moment
that's what seems to be on the cards.

He turns to LEDVOR.

                    ISAAC
          I want two plates of fish. A large beer...
          and a lime and soda for the lady. Make it
          snappy.

There is no way GUNNAR is going to allow ISAAC to
throw around orders in this manner.

                    GUNNAR
          That's enough. It's time to leave.

                    ISAAC
          I'm not going anywhere.

GUNNAR places a massive hand on ISAAC'S shoulder.

                    GUNNAR
          Time... to... leave.

ISAAC sees red. He slaps GUNNAR's hand away with
the back of one hand and throws a punch with the
other.

But GUNNAR has surprising agility to match
his size, and apparently plenty of brawling
experience. He calmly steps around the over-
committed punch, catches ISAAC's arm to pull him

off balance, then steps behind ISAAC to twist the
arm up his back and slam him down onto the bar
counter.

ISAAC's face plants sideways into the brass drip
tray as he hits the bar. He is bent double,
trapped in an arm lock, completely under GUNNAR's
control.

EMMA rushes over and pulls at GUNNAR's arm,
ignoring her condition in the panic of the
moment. She is close to tears.

                    EMMA
          STOP! PLEASE! LET HIM GO!

ISAAC tries to wriggle but cries out in pain as
GUNNAR pushes his twisted arm further.

                    GUNNAR
          OK boy, we don't need to fight. If I
          release you, will you agree to leave
          quietly and go back to wherever the hell
          you came from?

                    EMMA
          He IS back where he came from! But I can
          see why he left if this is the kind of
          welcome...

GUNNAR is perplexed by this reply.

                    GUNNAR
          What?

                    EMMA
          He's back where he came from. He was born
          here.

                    GUNNAR
                   (To ISAAC)
        You were... born here?

                    ISAAC
        (Grunts through the pain, teeth gritted)
        Yeah... YES!

                    GUNNAR
        What's your name?

                    ISAAC
        ISAAC!

                    GUNNAR
                  (Twists harder)
        Your family name! What's your family name?

                    ISAAC
        PICKMAN!

GUNNAR shakes his head and sneers.

                    GUNNAR
                  (Sarcastic)
        Pick - Man. Very Norwegian.

                    LEDVOR
        Most nights we can't move in here for all
        the Pickmans.

                    EMMA
        Jorstad! His birth-name was Jorstad.

                    GUNNAR
        Isaac... Jorstad...? Johan Jorstad's son?

                    ISAAC
        Yeah!

                    GUNNAR
        ISAAC JORSTAD!Why didn't you just say so?

He releases ISAAC's arm, hauls him to his feet by
his shoulders and spins him around so they are
facing each other. The corner of ISAAC's eyebrow
is bleeding where his head hit the bar, and he
rubs his recently tortured shoulder in obvious
pain.

                    GUNNAR (CONT'D)
                    (Apologetic)
        Your head is bleeding! Ledvor fetch the
        man a band aid. Sorry about... messing
        with you like that before. There's not
        much to do around here.

                    LEDVOR
                    (Embarrassed)
        Sleepy town. Restless sleep. You know how
        it is.

GUNNAR gestures to a young man at the other
corner of the bar.

                    GUNNAR
        MIKKEL! Don't just stand there! Get the
        lady a chair. Can't you see she is with
        child!

MIKKEL springs off his chair and drags it over to
EMMA.

                    GUNNAR
        And two plates of hake and a lime and
        soda! You're going to love it! The best
        hake in the whole of Norway - and that
        means, the best in the universe!

LEDVOR starts pouring EMMA'S drink into a frosted

glass stuffed with ice cubes and lime slices.
GUNNAR turns to ISAAC.

                    GUNNAR (CONT'D)
          What's your poison?

                    ISAAC
          Er... a beer please.

                    GUNNAR
          Beer? Pfff. Aquavit! Bring the bottle!

GUNNAR rests a giant meaty hand on the shoulders
of both ISAAC and EMMA.

                    GUNNAR (CONT'D)
          Tonight, we celebrate!

34   INT. RENATE HOUSE. DINING ROOM.34

RENATE, EMMA and ISAAC sit at the dining table.
It looks resplendent.

Dish after dish rests on fine silver plates.

> EMMA
> This all looks amazing!

ASTRID stands over ISAAC as she pours red wine
into his crystal goblet.

> ISAAC
> If it tastes as good as it looks...

He tries hard not to stare as she leans over him.
He nervously clears his throat.

> ISAAC (CONT'D)
> We're in for a treat...

EMMA watches him- trying not to watch ASTRID. She
redirects her attention to RENATE.

> RENATE
> It's all Astrid. I don't know where she
> inherited her domestic talents from...
> certainly not her mother!

> EMMA
> I must say I feel underdressed. You both
> look so glamorous.

> RENATE
> Don't be silly. Astrid and I don't get
> much opportunity to entertain... It's just
> lovely to have the company. Come on. Dive
> in. Before it gets cold.

EMMA takes a mouthful of food.

Her eyes light up in genuine pleasure.

                    EMMA
          That... that is absolutely divine. What
          have you put in this?

ASTRID stares back at her blankly.

                    RENATE
          I'm afraid Astrid doesn't talk much. Not
          since her father was taken from us.

                    EMMA
          Oh..

Beat.

                    RENATE
          So... when is the little one due?

                    EMMA
          Six weeks - we're well into the third
          trimester.

                    RENATE
          And will the child be born here?

                    EMMA
          Here? No! No...no. We're just here to make
          arrangements for the house. We need to
          head back in a couple weeks - while I'm
          still allowed to fly.

EMMA catches ASTRID gazing at ISAAC intently.

ISAAC looks intensely uncomfortable at being so
blatantly stared at by such a beautiful woman-
especially considering his pregnant wife is
sitting right by his side.

136

He offers ASTRID a bashful smile and then looks
down at his food.

EMMA tries to look anywhere but at ASTRID.

Her eyes latch onto the striking bronze plaque
hanging on the wall directly behind RENATE.

Once again it's a depiction of the tentacled sea
creature we have been seeing everywhere, only a
particularly aggressive rendition of it.

                    EMMA (CONT'D)
          That's a very- striking piece of art.

RENATE turns to look at the plaque behind her and
smiles proudly.

She looks back at EMMA.

                    RENATE
          Thank you! It's been with my family for
          generations.

                    EMMA
          What does the writing say?

                    RENATE
                  (Old Norse)
          "Tré skuggans a strond hússins hinna
          dauou". Old Norse.

EMMA nods blankly.

                    RENATE (CONT'D)
          "The tree of the shadow on the shores of
          the house of the dead".

                    EMMA
                  (Diplomatically)
          Okay...

                    RENATE
          But that's a lot to wrap your teeth
          around. Now we all just call him The
          Slumbering One.

                    EMMA
          The Slumbering One?

RENATE smiles.

                    RENATE
          Hinn sofandi. Local myth. Iceland has
          elves. Ireland has leprechauns. The rest
          of Norway has its trolls... and we have
          this lovely fellow.

EMMA is charmed by the whimsical nature of the
conversation.

                    EMMA
          So what does- The Slumbering One- do,
          exactly?

RENATE doesn't immediately answer. She seems to
be considering her question.

                    RENATE
          Not much, actually. The clue is in the
          name...

                    EMMA
          He sleeps?

                    RENATE
          Mostly, yes. Sometimes, he dreams.

                    EMMA
          Is that all?

Renate smiles.Shrugs.

                    RENATE
          I wish I could offer you something more
          exciting...

                    EMMA
          Maybe you should rename him 'The Lazy
          One'...

RENATE bursts out laughing.

                    RENATE
          Ha! Maybe we should!

RENATE seems equally as engaged in the discourse
and the company in general.

                    EMMA
          And the scarecrow in your garden?

                    RENATE
          We don't get too many crows here.
          Seagulls, of course, are another matter...

                    EMMA
          I assumed it was to scare something away.
          It's a little bit... sinister looking...
          if you don't mind me saying...

RENATE laughs again.

                    RENATE
          Ha! I certainly don't mind. Not at all. My
          husband on the other hand...

                    EMMA
          Your husband?

                    RENATE
          It's meant as a tribute to my late
          husband.

EMMA is deeply embarrassed by her gaffe.

                    EMMA
          Oh- I'm so sorry.

                    RENATE
                 (Melancholic)
          Mumtaz got the Taj Mahal...my husband got
          his sinister looking Tupilaq...

                    EMMA
          I'm so sorry. I didn't mean to offend you.
          It's dark outside. I'm sure it's very
          beautiful...

RENATE smiles at her with warm reassurance.

                    RENATE
          Don't be silly. You didn't offend in the
          slightest. And it's no prettier in the
          daylight. It's just another antiquated
          community custom. Dates back more years
          than we have counted. When a member
          is... taken from us... it is traditional
          to erect a Tupilaq in the image of The
          Slumbering One to celebrate the time we
          were permitted.

                    EMMA
          I see.

                    RENATE
          You'll see them scattered all over town,
          if you care to look. My husband was
          nothing if not a traditionalist.

EMMA nods her head sympathetically. ISAAC
forlornly cuts in.

                    ISAAC
                 (Mournful)
     Nobody built one of those to remember my
     dad...

This is more a melancholic statement rather
than a question. Now RENATE looks at ISAAC with
sympathetic eyes.

                    RENATE
     No... no they didn't.

There is a prolonged moment of silence. RENATE'S
demeanor suddenly changes.

A brightness re-enters her eyes.

                    RENATE (CONT'D)
     What have you both got planned for
     tomorrow?

                    EMMA
     Uh-

                    RENATE
     If you're interested in learning more
     about our community traditions, you should
     come and witness Altarisganga.

                    ISAAC
     Altaris- what?

                    RENATE
     Annual sacrament. I'm surprised you don't
     remember. I presided over all six of your
     Altarisganga when you were a child.

                    ISAAC
     Really?

                    RENATE
          Of course! Every year. And your mother.
          And your father... And just about
          everybody else who has called this place
          home for the last 30 years.

RENATE grins from ear to ear.

This is clearly something she is keen to show
them.

Colour of Madness Pictures Key

Colour of Madness 1: Filming begins in Essex on the underwater scenes, early summer 2019.

Colour of Madness 2: Male lead Ludovic Hughes as Isaac and Johanna Adde Dahl playing the character of Astrid, in the pool.

Colour of Madness 3: Johanna Adde Dahl.

Colour of Madness 4: An underwater shot is filmed.

Colour of Madness 5: Art Director Alex Jones Nash testing one of the tentacles being used.

Colour of Madness 6 & 7: Female lead Sophie Stevens as Emma filming the birth scene complete with dummy baby.

Colour of Madness 8: Co-director and co-writer Andy Collier, proud father.

Colour of Madness 9: Filming moves to the beautiful location of Bjorke, Norway.

Colour of Madness 10: A classic horror set-up with axe!

Colour of Madness 11: All hail Cthulhu! Some of the models made for the production.

Colour of Madness 12: Sophie Stevens as Emma, filming a scene in the shop.

Colour of Madness 13: Horror legend Barbara Crampton (Re-Animator, From Beyond) joins the cast as Renate.

Colour of Madness 14: Official production photo of leads Ludovic Hughes and Sophie Stevens.

Colour of Madness 15: Official production photo of Barbara Crampton.

Colour of Madness 16: Ludovic Hughes, who's been in the wars.

Colour of Madness 17: The cultists assemble!

Colour of Madness 18: Barbara Crampton sharing a laugh on set with Lukas Loughran, playing the character of Gunnar.

Colour of Madness 19: The night-time sacrificial fires are lit!

Colour of Madness 20: Barbara Crampton's Renate in contemplative mood.

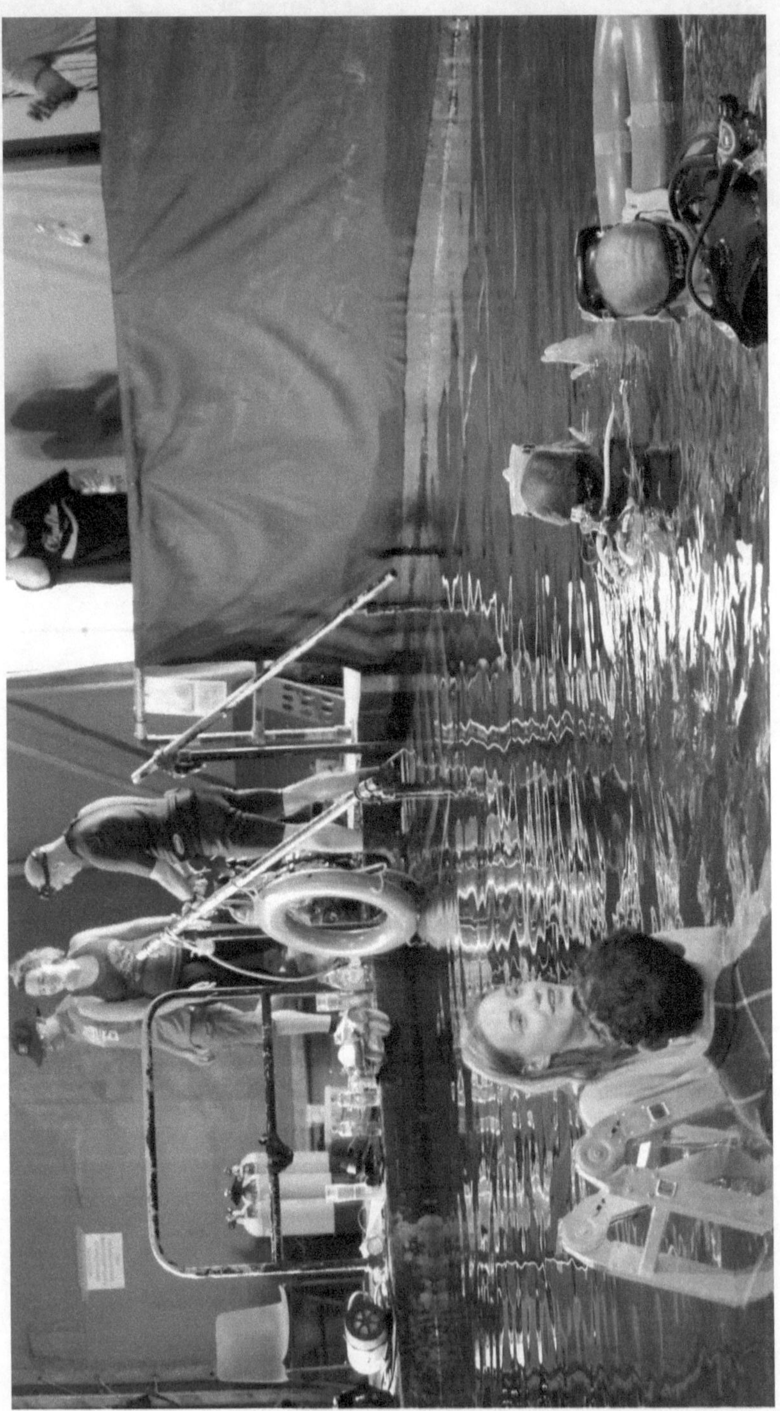

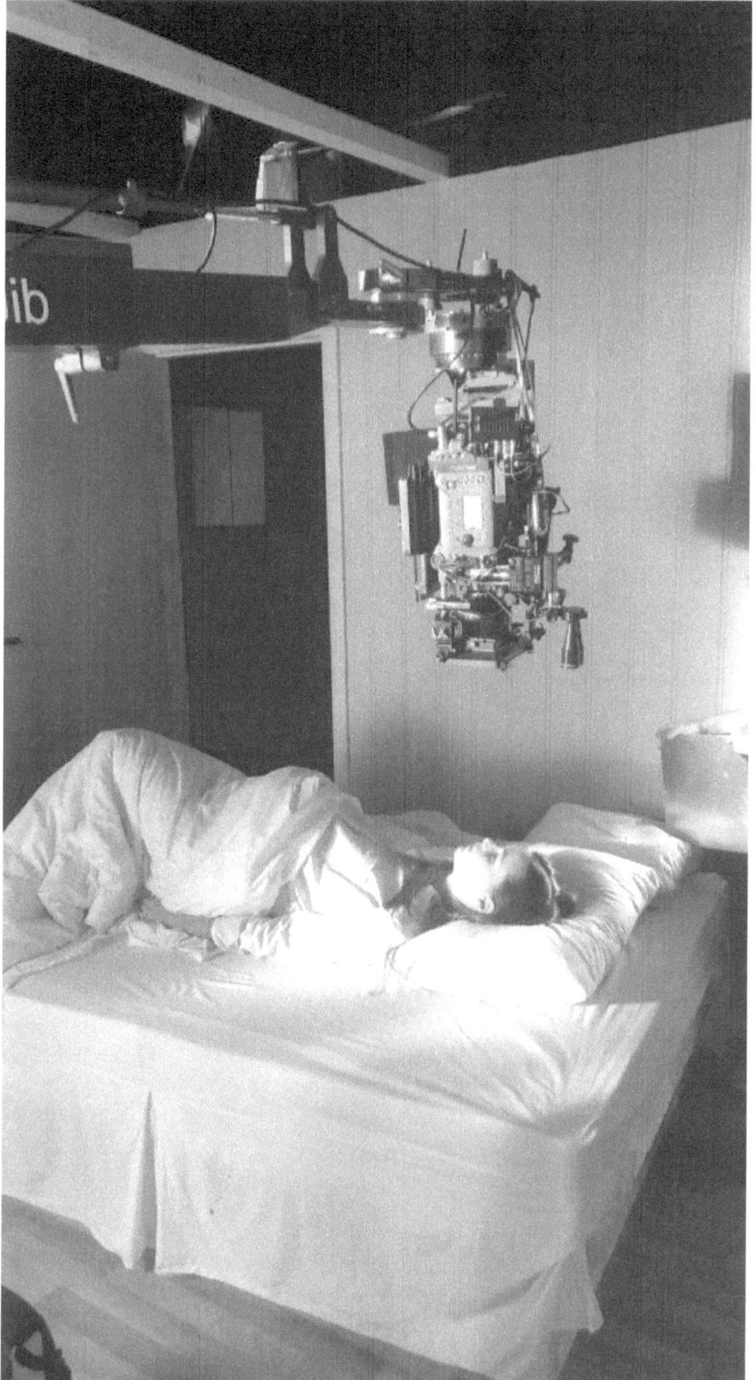
ib

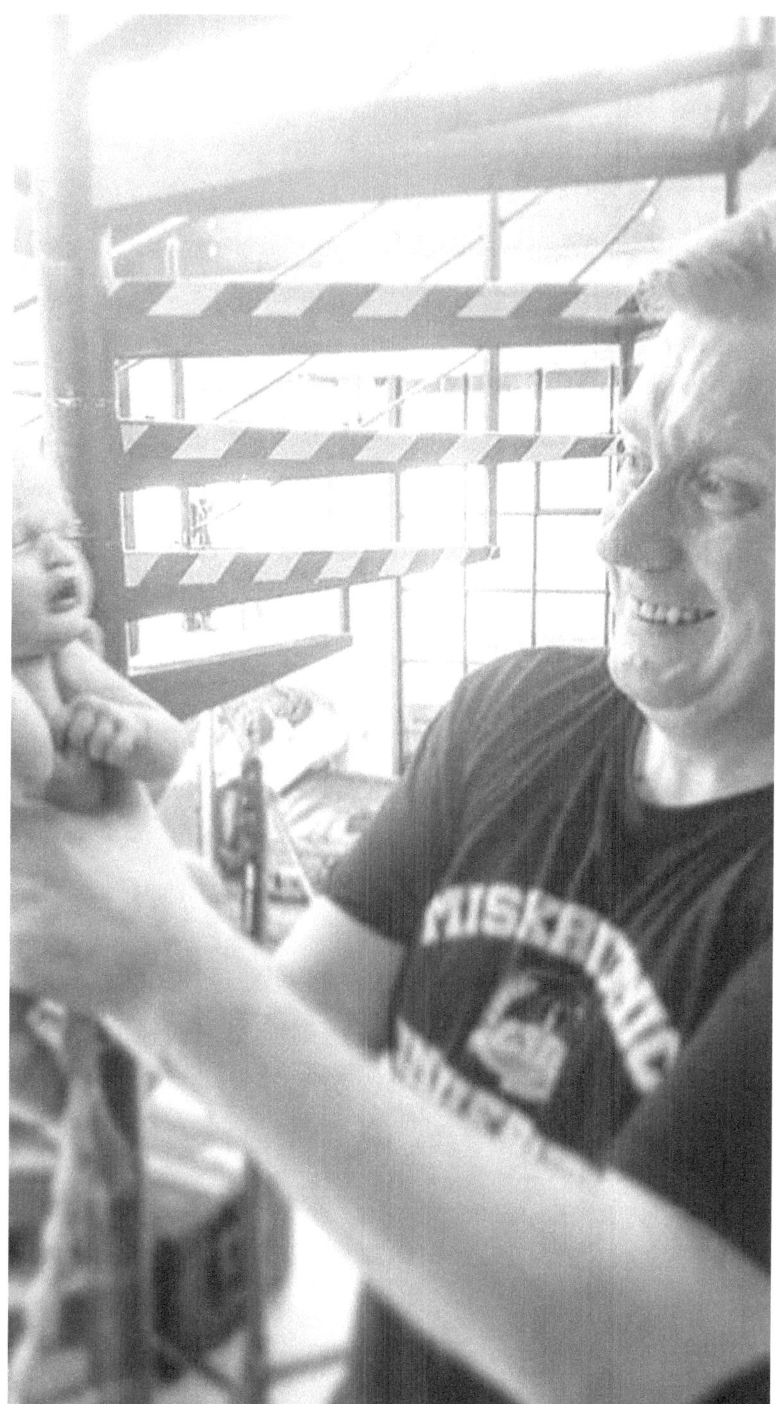

THE COLOUR OF MADNESS
CAM
628
SLATE 186
TAKE 1
#038
DATE 24/08/19

POLITI